MY LiFe
as a
Human Hockey Puck

BOOKS BY BILL MYERS

Children's Series
McGee and Me! (12 books)

The Incredible Worlds of Wally McDoogle
—*My Life As a Smashed Burrito with Extra Hot Sauce*
—*My Life As Alien Monster Bait*
—*My Life As a Broken Bungee Cord*
—*My Life As Crocodile Junk Food*
—*My Life As Dinosaur Dental Floss*
—*My Life As a Torpedo Test Target*
—*My Life As a Human Hockey Puck*
—*My Life As an Afterthought Astronaut*
—*My Life As Reindeer Roadkill*
—*My Life As a Toasted Time Traveler*
—*My Life As Polluted Pond Scum*

Fantasy Series
Journeys to Fayrah:
—*The Portal*
—*The Experiment*
—*The Whirlwind*
—*The Tablet*

Teen Series
Forbidden Doors:
—*The Society*
—*The Deceived*
—*The Spell*
—*The Haunting*

Adult Books
Christ B.C.
Blood of Heaven

the incredible worlds of **Wally McDoogle**

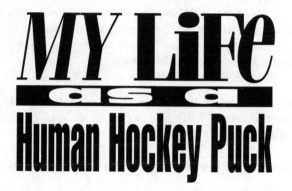

MY LiFe as a Human Hockey Puck

B I L L   M Y E R S

WORD PUBLISHING
Dallas·London·Vancouver·Melbourne

MY LIFE AS A HUMAN HOCKEY PUCK

Managing Editor: Laura Minchew
Project Editor: Beverly Phillips

Unless otherwise indicated, Scripture quotations are from the *International Children's Bible, New Century Version*, copyright © 1983, 1986, 1988.

Library of Congress Cataloging-in-Publication Data

Myers, Bill, 1953–
    My life as a human hockey puck / Bill Myers.
       p.   cm. — (The Incredible worlds of Wally McDoogle ; #7)

    Summary: Wally McDoogle as team mascot for the Middletown Super Chickens is calamity enough until he is also thrown in to play goalie.
    ISBN 0–8499–3601–2
    [1. Honesty—Fiction. 2. Christian life—Fiction. 3. Humorous stories.] I. Title. II. Series: Myers, Bill, 1953– Incredible worlds of Wally McDoogle ; #7.
PZ7.M98234Myh   1994
[Fic]—dc20   93-33671
                                             CIP
                                             AC

Printed in the United States of America

97 98 99 QBP 12

For Kristy and Terri—
Cousins and valued friends.

Peace of mind means a healthy body. But jealousy will rot your bones.

—Proverbs 14:30

Contents

Chapter 1

Just for Starters...

The nice thing about pain is that it comes in all sorts of sizes—from the...

Mini: "Excuse-me-you're-stepping-on-my-bare-feet-with-your-baseball-cleats" type of pain, to the...

Medium: "I-sure-wish-we-weren't-going-through-this-red-light-with-that-semitruck-coming-from-the-other-direction" type of pain, to the...

Maxi-Econo-Sized: "What-does-this-bully-mean-when-he-says-he's-about-to-give-me-some-free-dental-work?" type of pain.

Then, of course, there's the... **Giant, Industrial-Strength** version which I was about to experience....

We were playing flag football in co-ed P.E. when my old pal, Gary the Gorilla (who did not get his name by accident), broke through the line and came after our quarterback with all the gentleness of a locomotive gone crazy.

Our quarterback hesitated, looking very much like a deer caught in the headlights of a car. He spotted me out of the corner of his eye and shouted, "Hey, McDoogle, catch!"

Being no fool, he got rid of the ball as fast as he could.

Being a total fool, I caught it.

"Oh no," groaned Wall Street, one of my best friends (even though she is a girl).

I looked up to see Gary racing in my direction with his arms spread and a grin of major meanness across his face. Somehow I suspected he wasn't coming to give me a hug.

"Hey, Wall Street?" She was right beside me.

"Yeah, Wally?"

"How 'bout a handoff?"

"No thanks."

"Why not?"

"I'm allergic to death."

I looked back to Gary, who was still running toward us at full speed. "I see your point."

"Wally, should I use my cellular phone to call an ambulance?"

Gary was so close I could see the steam coming from his nostrils.

"You better make that a hearse."

Wall Street nodded and stepped out of the way. "Good luck."

Gary hit me. I'll save you all the gory details. Let's just say that even though it was flag football, Gary could never quite tell the difference between pulling out somebody's flag and scattering their body parts all over the field.

They scraped most of me up and poured me onto the sidelines next to Opera, my other best friend. As usual, he had a note from his mom forbidding him from any physical activity (other than eating junk food—and believe me, the way he chomps on those chips, it's definitely physical). His headphones were on and he was listening to classical stuff at a volume level just above "If This Doesn't Burst Your Eardrums, Nothing Will."

Coach Killroy didn't bother to check to see if I was okay. I'd been in his P.E. class for six months, and he was getting a little tired of bandaging me up, resetting my bones, and restarting my heart whenever I did anything athletic. It's not that I'm *un*athletic. The truth of the matter is, I'm really quite a jock. I'm even planning on participating in the Olympics . . . just as soon as they have an event for Stupendous Klutziness.

I looked down and saw Opera scribbling away in his notebook. "What are you doing?" I asked.

"What?" he shouted over his music.

I motioned to the paper.

"It's for the essay contest," he yelled. He tore off the sheet, crumpled it, and tossed it on top of a growing mountain of wadded paper beside him. "Mrs. Finkelstein is announcing the winners at the end of the day, and I still haven't got any ideas. What did you write about?"

Opera was referring to the sports essay contest WART-TV was holding. The winner would get to do the sports broadcasts for a whole week. Everybody was making a big deal about it. Everybody but me. I had it in the bag, and I knew it.

The way I figured, when God made me, He substituted all of my grace and coordination genes with writing ones. I may not be able to tie my shoes without ending up in an Intensive Care Unit, but believe me, I can write. So, of course I was going to win the writing contest. It was only fair. All I had to do was whip up something and hand it in before the end of the day. That was the easy part. Surviving P.E., well, that might be a little tougher. . . .

"Hey, McDoogle!" Coach Killroy shouted. "Can you walk yet?"

I looked at my legs, hoping they were missing, or at least broken into lots of little pieces. No such luck. They looked just as healthy as ever.

"Great," I moaned, "just great."

"Get in there and quarterback for a while," he ordered.

I rose unsteadily to my feet and looked at the other team. There were Gary the Gorilla and half a dozen of his overfed (and undereducated) goons dragging their bodies (and knuckles) up to the scrimmage line. There was no missing the gleam in their eyes and the saliva drooling out of the corners of their mouths as they anxiously waited to turn me into football shoe goo.

I turned back to Opera and shouted, "Why don't you write your story on hockey! You're a big hockey nut. Write about hockey."

"That's a great idea!" he shouted as he crumpled up his 1,234th piece of paper and started number 1,235. "Thanks."

I shrugged. It was no biggie. The way I figured, since I was on my way to meet God, I might as well squeeze in a final good deed to impress Him.

*   *   *   *   *

Twenty minutes later I limped down the hall toward my locker. Somehow, I had made it through another grueling class of P.E., which, as we all know, does NOT stand for *Physical Education*, but rather *Physical Embarrassment*.

Opera was still babbling on about the writing contest. "I can't believe you haven't started," he shouted over his Walkman while tearing into his second bag of chips.

"Wally's a pro," Wall Street said as she joined us from the girls' locker room. "Pros can do that sort of thing in their sleep, right Wally?"

Before I could shrug and fake some modesty, another voice drifted through the air. "Hiii, Waaally." It was as lovely as a spring day, as soft as a rose pedal, and as cunning as a carnival barker. I turned around to see Melissa Sue Avarice, the most beautiful girl in our school.

She smiled her perfect every-tooth-in-place smile and batted her baby blues in my direction. "I'm *really* looking forward to seeing *you* on TV, Wally."

I opened my mouth. It was time to play it suave and cool. Time to impress her with my wit and intelligence. "Daa, uhhh, I mean, ummmm, daaa, yeah, uhhh, sure." So much for wit and intelligence. Not only did her beauty tie my tongue, but it also seemed to be knotting my brain.

"What makes you so sure he's going to win?" Opera shouted over his music.

"Because he's *sooo* smart," Melissa cooed. "Besides, if he doesn't win, how will he take me to meet Vincent Thrasher, WART-TV's ultra-hunk anchorman?"

I nodded eagerly. "Daa, uhhh, I mean, ummmm, daaa . . ."

She gave me a pathetic look, the same type you give animals lying on the side of the freeway. She forced a smile and headed down the hall. "Good luck, Wally Dolly," she called over her shoulder.

"Daa, uhhh, ummm, daaa . . ."

Wall Street groaned, "*'Wally Dolly?'* Give me a break."

I nodded. "Daa, uhhh, ummm, daaa . . ."

Wall Street punched me in the gut. "Knock it off, she's just a girl."

I continued watching Melissa float down the hall. Finally my mouth started working. "That's no girl, Wall Street, that's poetry in motion. Melissa Sue Avarice is . . . well, she's . . . she's . . ."

Opera, who was also staring after her, finished the thought with a longing sigh. "She's an extra-large order of piping hot fries, covered in salt, and drenched in cool, dripping ketchup."

I nodded.

Wall Street looked from me to Opera. "Guys." And from Opera to me. "Guys?"

No response from either of us.

"Guys, she's nothing but a user."

"Exactly," we sighed in perfect two-part harmony.

"I can't believe you two are so blind."

"You're the one who is blind," I said, still dazed. "If you can't see past her shallow and superficial personality—"

"You left out, 'spoiled,'" Opera corrected. "Don't forget 'spoiled.'"

"Right. If you can't see past her shallow, selfish, *and spoiled* personality to appreciate that beautiful hair, that lovely face, those expensive clothes . . . then you're the one who is blind."

Wall Street glared at us, then she spun around and stormed down the hall, muttering all the way. She had just disappeared into the crowd when I heard another voice. "Hey, McDoogle!"

I could tell by the prehistoric accent that it was Bruno Pistarini—one of the dimmest bullies in school. I don't want to say he's stupid, but he's the only eighth-grader I know who's old enough to vote. "We gots some business ta takes care of!" he said.

One of the major problems of being the all-school punching bag and having your locker this close to a lavatory, is that whenever one of these semi-human types feels a little anxious, you may be called upon to help them relax. It's kind of a public service.

"Loan me your pad and pencil," I whispered to Opera. "Looks like I'm going to have some spare time to write that article."

"What about your laptop computer?"

"It's not waterproof."

Opera nodded and quickly handed me his pad and pencil. Then, doing his best to look casual, he slowly turned, tried to whistle (not an easy task with half a bag of potato chips in your mouth), and ran down the hallway screaming for his life.

You really couldn't blame him. For some people, living can be a habit that's really hard to break. Unfortunately, I don't have that problem.

Suddenly a hand the size of Seattle grabbed my collar and hoisted me into the air. As Bruno threw me over his shoulder and hauled me down the hall, I flipped open the notepad and began to write. It wouldn't be my best work, with all of the distractions and everything, but at least it would help take my mind off the upcoming pain.

As usual, Bruno kicked open the locker room door. *BAMB!*

As usual, I was greeted by the kids suiting up for next period's P.E.:

"Hey, Wally . . . How's it going, McDoogle . . . Good luck on that essay contest."

I nodded and continued writing.

Bruno entered the bathroom and kicked open the stall door. *BANG!*

Suddenly, I was turned upside down and held dangling by my ankles. But, before the fun and games really got started, I cleared my throat. "Uh, Bruno?"

"What?" He sounded as brain dead as ever.

"Would you mind holding off for just a second? I'm almost done writing this essay."

"Well, hurry, I ain't got all day."

I nodded and scribbled away.

"Aren't ya done yet?"

"Just about." I completed the last sentence with a flair and dotted the period. "Thanks, Bruno, you're a pal."

"Don't mention it." With that he opened the toilet lid, pushed down the flush lever . . . *SWOOOOSH!* . . . and stuck my head into the swirling water.

Ah yes, the ever-popular "Swirlie." One of my favorites. The good news was I had finished the article. It only took a minute and twenty-three seconds to write. And, as usual, it was great. But not as great as it was going to be to appear for a solid week on WART-TV with the ever-beautiful Melissa Sue Avarice waiting for me in the wings. How lucky could a guy get? *SWOOOOSH!*

Oh boy, a double-header. I really was lucky.

Chapter 2

And the Winner Isn't...

After taking a few more laps around the toilet, I swung by the office and dropped off my essay. It was a little wet around the edges, but still readable, and still pretty good.

I pulled ol' Betsy, my laptop computer, out of my locker and headed to the library for study hall. Mr. Hackelburn, the librarian, didn't notice me as I slipped into the chair beside Opera.

This was the last period of the day. Since I only had about four zillion hours of homework ahead of me, I figured I'd waste some time with another one of my superhero stories. I popped open Betsy's lid, snapped her on, and began to write. . . .

It had been another boring day of outer space superherohood for the ever-

11

so-magnificent Macho Man McDoogle. Already he had captured and returned Saturn's rings (someone was trying to sell them as giant Hula Hoops), plugged up two black holes (a job that took more than your average mouthful of chewing gum), and finally learned the real words to "The Star-Spangled Banner" (although he's still not sure what "twilight's last screaming" means).

Now he is on the distant planet "ThisGetsStrangerYet," trying not to yawn during a parade they are holding in his honor. Why are they making such a big deal? All he did was save their world from total destruction. All he did was toss a couple of nuclear bombs in the path of a runaway asteroid that was about to turn them all into intergalactic roadkill. Why all the fuss?

Who knows. But, here he sits, high atop a float, waving his marvelously manly arms to his adoring fans. Of course, it's hard to see over his gigantic rippling muscles. And every time he flexes, his bulging biceps rip out his XXXX-Large shirt. But it's a small price to pay for being the strongest man in the universe.

Suddenly a rare Three-headed Bubble-brain breaks through the cheering crowd. "Oh Macho Man, Macho Man—you're so strong, you're so brave, you're so... so..."

"Macho?" Macho Man smiles.

"Yes," she sighs, "*Macho*. And I love you sooo much."

"Of course you do," Macho Man grins while striking a manly pose. "What's not to love? These tremendously thick triceps? These larger-than-life thighs?" He wiggles his toes, and they tear through his shoes. "Even these tremendous tootsies are terrifically tough."

The crowd goes wild. They've never seen such staggering strength (or cheap shoes). They surge forward, racing into the street, climbing onto his float, trying to touch him. First there are the seven-legged Fallerdowners (you'd fall down too if you had to keep track of seven legs), then the four-armed Chestthumpers, and finally the ever-unpopular Burperbreaths. It's the Burperbreaths our hero fears the most. They are everywhere.

"Oh Macho Man *(BURP)*, Macho Man. I'm *(BURP)* your biggest *(BELCH)* fan."

"Of course you are," Macho Man says, quickly backing away from their toxic breath. The fumes are already starting to melt the plastic rims of Macho Man's glasses. He rises to his feet and climbs higher up the float for some fresh air.

"Macho *(BURP)* Man, Macho *(BELCH)* Man..."

They surround him from every side, climbing after him. Closer and closer they come.

BURP, BELCH, BURP.

Higher and higher he climbs.

BELCH, BURP, BEEEEEEEEEEEELCH (that was a good one).

And then, just when it looks like Macho Man has no place to go, just when it looks like he'll have to hold his breath for eternity (or call for an air tanker to drop a load of Listerine), everything freezes.

That's right, everything stops—the float, the crowd, even the Burperbreaths. Everything is frozen. Everything but Macho Man.

He looks around. "Hello?"

No answer. No sound. No one moves.

"Can anybody hear me?"

Repeat performance.

"Excuse me? Hello..."

He stops and flexes his brawny biceps. If that doesn't get a rise out of the crowd, nothing will.

Nothing does.

He climbs down the float—past the Burperbreaths who no longer burp, past the Chestthumpers who no longer thump, and past the seven-legged Fallerdowners who no longer fall but are frozen in midair.

"Doesn't anybody hear me? What's going on?"

Panic suddenly seizes our sizable superhero. How can he live without adoring crowds, without screaming fans? What fun is it being the marvelous Macho Man if no babes are fainting in your presence, if weaker guys aren't turning green with envy? Is it possible that he's doomed to stroll the universe alone, never to be worshiped again?

And then, just when he's deciding whether to pinch himself to see if he's dreaming, or throw himself down and have a good macho cry, he hears it—a voice echoing through his head. "Greetings, Midget Mind."

Our hero gasps a manly gasp. He rec-
ognizes the voice instantly. It's the
sinister Time Trickster. The diabolical scientist who tricks people with
time. No one's sure what made this mad
scientist so mad. Some say it's because
he could never find his snooze alarm
button in the morning. Others say it was
from getting one too many digital wrist
watches for one too many Christmases.

"Where are you?" Macho Man cries.
"What have you done?"

"I have finally invented the ultimate
computer. A timepiece that controls all
other clocks in the universe."

"What do you mean?"

"Take a look at your watch, Bicep
Brain."

Our hero raises his muscular wrist to
his muscular face and gasps another
macho gasp. "The second hand, it's
stopped!"

"Precisely. I now control all time in
the universe."

"But..."

"And that's only the beginning. Look
at this!"

Suddenly, the second hand of our hero's
watch starts running backwards. But it's

not just his second hand. His feet are
also running backwards. He's climbing
back onto the float. The Burperbreaths
are climbing down. The Fallerdowers are
falling up. Everyone is moving backwards! Not only moving backwards, but
talking backwards!

"!naM *(HCLEB)* ohcaM ,naM *(PRUB)* ohcaM"
they cry as they back away from him and
return to the street curb.

".era uoy esruoc fO," Macho Man says
as he backs into his original position
on the float.

".naf *(HCLEB)* tseggib ruoy m'I .naM
(PRUB) ohcaM, *(PRUB)* naM ohcaM hO"

Great Scott! What will our superhero
do? Will he ever get time running forward again? Will he ever be adored again?
And, most importantly, will we have to
read the rest of this story's dialogue
in a mirror?

These are the questions running through
our pumped-up, superbod, good guy, when
suddenly—

"Attention please . . . attention . . ."
It was the school PA system. There was a loud
squeal of feedback. That meant the microphone

was in the clumsy hands of Vice Principal Watkins, who never could get the hang of using the school's intercom. I shut ol' Betsy down and saved the rest of my Macho Man story for another time.

"Attention please . . . SQUEAL . . . Our seventh grade English teacher, Mrs. Finkelstein, has just completed the judging of the entries for the WART-TV essay contest.

I threw a look over to Opera. For some reason he had stopped eating. In fact, he was actually holding his breath and staring at the speaker in nervous anticipation. I couldn't believe my eyes. Did he actually think he'd have a chance?

Don't get me wrong, Opera has his own set of talents. And we were all looking forward to seeing him become the first classical-singing sumo wrestler. But writing? Forget it. The only writing Opera did was a shopping list. Even then all he had to spell was: *chips, chocolate,* and *cookies.*

"Mrs. Finkelstein would like to say . . . SQUEAL . . . that all the entries were outstanding and she wishes all of them could . . . SQUEAL . . . could represent our school. Well, all except the one describing the joys of biting off lizard heads—would Bruno Pistarini please make an appointment to visit the school counselor as soon as possible? In any case . . . SQUEAL . . . the winning representative for Olympic Heights Middle School is . . . "

I braced myself, preparing for the onslaught of congratulations. . . .

"*Mr. Oliver 'Opera' Livingston!*"

I started rising to my feet and giving a humble wave to my adoring fans. Then I caught myself. What did he say?

"*Congratulations, Opera. We'll all be listening to the news tonight, as you compete against the other schools. We all hope you'll be the* . . . SQUEAL . . . *winner. Good luck!*"

I don't remember much after that. It seems there was a bunch of commotion and back-slapping near Opera. I vaguely heard his voice shouting, "All right, free chips for everybody!" and finally the distant sound of the school bell ringing.

"Hey, Wally . . . Wally . . ." The next thing I knew, Opera was shaking me. "Are you okay? Are you all right?"

"Huh? Oh yeah, uh, sure." I rubbed my forehead and started gathering my books. "I tell you, I just had the weirdest dream. I dreamed that you were the guy who won the—"

"Have a chip." He shoved the salt-saturated grease under my nose. "They're on the house."

"I, uh, I don't . . ."

"Isn't this fantastic?" He grabbed his books and turned toward the door. "I think I'm going down to my safe-deposit box at the bank and withdraw my private stock of Super-Duper, Double-Fried Salties to celebrate. Want to come?"

My head reeled. It hadn't been a dream. Somehow Opera had won. Somehow he had beaten me. And worst of all, he had beaten me with an idea I had given him!

I'm not sure how I got to my feet, but soon we were heading toward the exit. As we arrived, I looked up, and there she was . . . Melissa Sue Avarice—waiting for me at the door. Once again she was smiling that perfect, heartbreaking smile.

Suddenly my pain vanished. Suddenly the agony of defeat was gone. All it took was that beautiful smile. What joy and comfort to know there was still somebody who stayed by my side through thick and thin, good or bad, win or—

"Hi, Opera," she chirped while batting her baby blues at him.

Opera's mouth fell open. He was as surprised as I was.

"I'm just so thrilled that you won, aren't you?"

"Well, uh, yeah," he sort of squeaked, "sure . . ."

Before I knew it, she had wrapped her arm around his, escorted him through the door, and led him down the hall. I could only stare.

"Great," I sighed in disbelief, "just great." What else could go wrong?

"Hey, McDoogle." It was Bruno's voice. Then it was Bruno's hand around my collar. "I'm still feelin' a little tense—let's you and me swing by da lavatory."

It's good to know there are still some people you can always rely on.

Chapter 3

Time for a Change

There's a trick to eating my little sister's cooking.
You don't.

When it's Carrie's turn to fix dinner, just make sure you smuggle all sorts of empty containers to the table—something to stuff and hide her so-called 'food' into. Empty bags, cassette cases, business envelopes—anything will do, just as long as Carrie doesn't see you.

I don't want to say her cooking is bad, but even our pet cat, Collision (who did not get her name for her brilliance) stays out from under the table on those nights. And it isn't just to avoid eating the fallen scraps. When those scraps hit the floor, there's no telling which direction they'll bounce or how much damage they'll do when they hit.

Carrie was passing around her wanna-be food, insisting everyone have seconds on her French-fried spinach and candied Brussels sprouts. Fortunately, the TV news was blaring loudly. Carrie looked away as they headlined the news about the contest finalists, and she didn't notice us shoveling the "delectable" goodies away.

"Isn't this exciting?" Mom said. "Opera, your very own friend, a finalist right here on the news."

"Yeah," I said, while stuffing something that looked like a cross between frozen frog eyes and lizard eggs into a plastic baggie, "just great."

"You don't sound too thrilled," Dad commented.

I shrugged and kept stuffing. What could I say? That Mrs. Finkelstein picked the wrong essay? That I should be the finalist? Of course it was true, but how do you put that into words? Fortunately, my older brother Brock saved me the trouble.

"Couldn't be you're a little jealous, could it Wally?" he taunted.

I looked up and glared. Me? Jealous? Of what? I could feel my face start to get red, like it always does when I get mad.

Brock broke into a semi-toothless grin (a reminder of last football season where he blocked one too many kicks). He had me and he knew it. I *was* jealous. *Real* jealous. But of whom? Of my best friend? A fellow Dork-oid? What a terrible thought.

"Check it out!" said Burt, my other brother. He was just as much a jock as Brock and had just as many missing teeth. He motioned to the TV, where the sportscaster was talking about our new minor league hockey team, the Super Chickens. They were holding tryouts next week and everyone was invited.

They cut to Coach Krashenburn (formerly of Krashenburn's Used Cars) who was saying, "I believe we've got plenty of local talent right here in this local community. So I look forward to every local kid coming on down to show me what he's got!"

Burt and Brock exchanged glances.

"What do you say, Brock?"

"You mean us trying out, Burt?"

"That's right, Brock."

"I'm with you, Burt."

They high fived and resumed stuffing their shirt pockets with my sister's blackeyed peas, which had the look and taste of overcooked sand.

And then it happened. The announcement everyone had been waiting for . . .

"Well, it was a close call," the sports commentator was saying, "and we at WART-TV want to thank every school for participating. But the essay that best captured the thrill and excitement of sports came from Olympic Heights Middle School."

Suddenly Opera's photo appeared behind the sportscaster. Of course it was upside down and backwards (WART-TV never had money to hire real professionals). But there was no missing my best friend, standing there on his head, grinning away at us!

"All right!" Dad shouted.

"Way to go, Opera!" Mom cried.

"Everybody ready for dessert?" Carrie asked. "It's cauliflower cobbler."

I don't remember what happened next. Except I somehow avoided the cauliflower cobbler and wound up in my room. I was stewing. I was more than stewing, I was steaming. I was more than steaming, I was boiling, I was more than—that's enough cooking symbolism, you probably get the point.

How could I, the gifted writer, have lost to that . . . that . . . Overeater's Anonymous reject! It just wasn't fair. Writing was *my* speciality. Let the others have the girls, the brains, the athletics. I was a writer. That was my niche, *MY* speciality.

As I sat on the bed brooding, I could feel my stomach tying into little knots. Square knots, hitch knots, slipknots—you name it, I tied it. I was experiencing jealousy in the first degree.

I kept thinking, "It's not fair. I've got to show them. How can I show them?" And then it hit me like a freight train (actually a freight train would have done less damage). If Opera thinks he can write, let him write. Let him do that stupid sportscast. See what I care. If everybody thinks he's such a great writer, big deal. I would find a new niche. I would find something no one else could do. And I would do it better than Opera or any of them ever dreamed of doing it. That would show him. That would show all of them.

But what? The only thing I was good at was writing . . . and serving as the all-school punching bag. But there had to be something. I grabbed a piece of paper and started a list. I knew there was something out there, and I knew I would find it.

*   *   *   *   *

"Good morning!" the all-too-cheery disk jockey greeted me over my radio alarm. *"It's another beautiful day here in Middletown and time for all you sleepyheads to rise and shine."*

I rolled over in bed and looked at the clock. It read:

6:33 AM

I fumbled for my glasses and put them on. Now it read:

6:33 AM

That was better, but not by much. I'd been up all night working on my list of "New Opportunities." Having only squeezed in a couple hours of sleep, I was a little on the cranky side. Mr. Over-Cheery Announcer did not help:

"And, hey, we just want to wish a hearty congratulations to Opera Livingston for winning that essay contest last night . . ."

"Wonderful," I sighed, "is there anybody in the whole world who doesn't know?"

"We're really looking forward to seeing you on the air, little buddy."

I snapped off the radio and staggered to my closet. I slipped into some pants but couldn't find the zipper. Then I realized I had them on backwards. After changing them around, I threw on yesterday's shirt (not at all bothered by the candied Brussels sprouts that tumbled out of the pocket), and slumped down behind my desk to review the New Opportunities list.

Immediately I could tell that some ideas were flat out wrong. Take for instance:

NUCLEAR SCIENTIST—A great job, but I can't sleep with a light glowing in the room. Especially if it happens to be me.

TRAPEZE ARTIST—Fun and excitement. But, as you may recall from my little hot-air balloon adventure, I'm afraid of heights. Actually, it's not the heights I'm afraid of; it's the lows. It can really be depressing when you're the one making the depression . . . in the ground.

TOOTHBRUSH MAKER—I don't think my hands are small enough to fit in there and poke all those little bristles into all their little holes.

I crossed these and a couple hundred other ideas off the list before I packed up and headed to school.

Classes were kind of a blur. But if I heard one more kid tell me how great it was that my best friend would get on WART-TV, I'd . . . well, I don't know what I'd do, but it wouldn't be pretty. Of course, Opera tried to talk to me about a million times, but I was always too busy. I tell you, jealousy was really eating into me, and there didn't seem to be any way to stop it.

By the end of the day I had my list narrowed down to three topics. Three completely different images for the *New And Improved Wally McDoogle*. I would spend the next few days making the rounds, testing them out, figuring which would be the best for me to pursue.

On Wednesday it was:

WALLY MCDOOGLE, BALLET DANCER . . .

I found a pretty cool ballet school and signed up. I really didn't mind the tights or those sissy slippers. And there could be worse problems than being the only guy surrounded by about two hundred babes. It's just when those two hundred babes started leaping into the air, expecting me to catch them that I got a little tense.

I did all right at the beginning. I even managed to catch 68-pound Nicole and 72-pound Heather. It was when I saw 164-pound Susan flying at me that I had second thoughts.

My teacher, Ms. Stanaslobsky, showed no pity. As soon as they pulled Susan off me and peeled my body from the floor, she dragged me over to a long bar about chest-high that was in front of a mirror.

"Ond now Master McDoogle, ve vill verk on vlexibilty."

"What's that?" I asked.

"Virst, ve put your right leg up on de bar like zo." She grabbed my right leg and threw it over the bar. I had no idea it could go so high. "Ond den ve bend down wit de oder knee like zo."

"But . . ." I wanted to say it was impossible. You can't stretch a person in two different directions at the same time. I signed up to be a dancer, not a Gumby doll. But before I could get the words out, she grabbed my shoulders and pushed down.

"Augh!" I cried.

"Nonzense, Master McDoogle," she said as she kept pushing, "de body, she lufs to stretch."

"Augh! Augh!" I cried.

"A lettle pain in de beginning iz good. And in de end you vill feel zo much—"

RIIIIPPP!

"Vhat vas dat?" she asked. "Vas dat your leotards ripping?"

"No ma'am," I groaned. "That was my leg."

She looked down and scowled. "Amazink. I haf never seen anyzing like dat."

Everyone watched as she eased my leg off the bar and helped me hobble across the floor. The pain was bad, but not as bad as having a left leg that was now three inches longer than my right. Later, as they rolled me and my new wheelchair out the door, I began to think dancing may not be my cup of tea.

The next day it was:

WALLY MCDOOGLE, BRAIN SURGEON

Obviously school wasn't the way to go. If you felt that type of pain just learning to dance, imagine what type of pain you'd have learning to dig around in some guy's brain. No sir, I figured it was time for a little on-the-job training.

No one noticed me sneaking into Middletown General Hospital. And no one was in the scrub room when I sneaked inside, found a gown, and washed and suited up. By the time I put on the face mask, along with my Woody Allen glasses, I could pass for any midget-sized adult (as long as they didn't hear my kid-sized voice).

I found an operation just getting started so I slipped inside the operating room. I was a little disappointed that I didn't get to be the guy doing the cutting, but, hey, it wouldn't hurt to watch the first time, just to get the hang of things.

And then it happened . . .

The head surgeon called out, "Dr. Theo?"

No one answered.

"Dr. Theo?"

Still no answer. I glanced around the room, looking for the good doctor.

"Dr. Theo, please, we need more sedation!"

Everyone looked up. Unfortunately they were all looking up at *me*. "Dr. Theo, we need more anesthetic." The surgeon nodded toward the three tanks at my side. "Please, he's starting to regain consciousness."

I had this incredible sinking feeling. It looked like everyone thought I was Dr. Theo. And by the sound of things, Dr. Theo was the guy responsible for keeping the patient asleep during the operation. Don't ask me how the mix-up happened (although the fact that Dr. Theo's nametag was attached to the gown I had borrowed probably didn't help).

Trying to look very official, I scowled and shook my head at the surgeon.

"Don't tell me no," he snapped. "Look at those readouts." He motioned to a bunch of monitors with a bunch of numbers. "Start administrating that gas now!" Ol' Doc was about to blow a gasket. He definitely expected me to do something with those three tanks beside me. I looked at them. Each had different letters and numbers on them.

"Doctor!" he ordered. "Now!"

I had to act. I had to turn on one of those tanks. But which one? Luckily, the solution was simple. I asked myself, which tank would Wally McDoogle *NOT* choose. Once I decided that, I made sure that was the tank I *DID* choose. (As a walking disaster area, you learn these little tricks of the trade.)

I reached over to the chosen tank and nervously turned on the valve. It gave a quiet hiss. I wasn't sure what to do next, but it didn't matter, because the nurse beside me suddenly started to giggle.

"Dr. Theo, *he-he-he,* what have you done?"

I shrugged and for some reason started giggling myself.

The doctor to my right looked up and also started to chuckle. "Dr. Theo . . . *har-har-har* . . . you've turned on the . . . *har-har-har* . . . wrong tank."

Others looked up. They were also starting to giggle. Even the head surgeon gave a little chuckle, and then another, and another, until he was really yucking it up. "Dr. Theo, *ho-ho-ho,* you've, *ha-ha-*

ha, you've . . ." he tried to get the words out, but he was laughing so hard he could barely breathe. "You've turned on the laughing gas!"

Everyone burst out laughing. The nurses had to lean against the table to hold themselves up. Assistants were grabbing their sides. We were all splitting a gut, and there was nothing we could do to stop. Everyone roared. Tears streamed down our faces. We held our stomachs. Some dropped to their knees, doubling over, unable to catch their breath. Others pointed at my tank, laughing so hard they were crying like babies.

Yes sir, I was definitely the life of the party. A real crack-up . . . until one of the nurses managed to drag herself to the tank (laughing all the way), pull herself up to the valve, and finally shut it off.

The effects of the laughing gas quickly came to an end . . . so did my career as a surgeon.

I had one option left:

WALLY MCDOOGLE, SUPER BOWLER

Unfortunately, that career was even shorter-lived. It started and ended with my first bowling lesson. I was the perfect student. I took the right amount of steps, slid my foot the right way, and I even threw the ball with a perfect spin. Unfortunately no one told me I was supposed to let go.

I flew down the alley. Of course it was a strike. But, by the time they called 911 and brought in the welder to cut me out of the pin-setting machine, I knew bowling wasn't my calling, either.

But what? What could I do?

And then, as luck would have it, just as I stepped out of the bowling alley, there were my older brothers Burt and Brock. They're twins.

"Hey, Wally, where are you going?"

I shrugged.

"Why don't you come with us," Burt suggested.

"Yeah," Brock agreed. "Come over and watch us try out for that hockey team."

"You're going to try out for the Super Chickens?"

"Yeah, come on."

I'd participated in enough disasters for one week. I figured it wouldn't hurt to kick back and watch somebody else get their lickings for a change.

As usual, I couldn't have been more wrong. . . .

Chapter 4

Mad Dog and Me

When my brothers and I entered the ice rink it was just like old times. There were all my old bully buddies skating and running drills.

Gary the Gorilla was the first to spot me. "Hey, Dork-oid, how's it going?"

I waved.

Next, Bruno Pistarini yelled, "McDorkel, wait'll you see the toilets in this shower room." He gave me the thumbs up. "They're primo."

I nodded. "I can hardly wait."

Then there was Coach Krashenburn. He looked a lot smaller in real life than on TV, but he was just as sweet and charming when he shouted at us, "You punks are late! Get your rears out here, and let's see what you've got!"

My brothers immediately kicked off their shoes and started lacing up their skates. I immediately started for the bleachers.

"Hey, you! Kid!"

I stopped and turned. He was yelling at me. "I told you to get out here!"

"But—"

"Now!"

"But, but—"

"You got a problem with that?"

"But, but, but—"

"Hey, Arnie!"

A short, fat man with bright red hair appeared from behind the bleachers. "Yeah, boss?"

"Doesn't look like the kid's got skates."

Arnie glanced at me and scowled. "We don't got children's sizes."

"Then get him a pair of ladies'."

"Right, boss."

"But Coach Krashenburn," I tried to explain, "I'm not a hockey player. I've never been on skates in my life!"

"Don't let him fool you, Coach." It was Gary the Gorilla, looking for a little fun. "He may be small, but he's quick."

"That's right," Bruno jumped in with his own mischievous grin. "The kid's as fast as lightning."

"Come on, guys," I protested, but others were also getting into the act, saying how great and fast I was. I turned to my brothers. I knew they'd set the coach straight. And being the kind, thoughtful fellows they are, they nodded and said, "That's right, Coach—he taught us everything we know." The team laughed. Everyone got the joke except Coach Krashenburn. Before I knew it, I was holding a white pair of ladies' skates (complete with little pink pom-poms tied to the laces).

"Get out here!" Krashenburn shouted. "Now!"

Resistance was futile. The best way to show him I couldn't skate would be . . . well, it would be to show him I couldn't skate. I sat down and put on the skates. When I finished I turned to Arnie. "Are you sure these are the right size? They're killing my feet."

"There's a good reason for that."

"What?"

"You've got them on the wrong feet."

"Oh right," I chuckled nervously, "I knew that." I had just finished relacing them when the entire building shook.

K-BAMB!

My eyes shot up to see one of the players slowly slide down the clear plastic wall in front of me. He was as unconscious as I usually am during science class. Another player, the size of a bulldozer, stood over the limp, bleeding body, gloating as if he'd just made some sort of big-game kill. Maybe he had."

"All right, Mad Dog!" Krashenburn shouted. "Nice check! Nice check!"

Mad Dog Miller said nothing. He just hovered over his victim while the tiniest trace of drool slobbered down his chin.

I saw my brothers exchange nervous glances. I saw everybody exchange nervous glances.

"Okay," Krashenburn shouted. "Who's going against Mad Dog next?"

I decided to relace my shoes.

There was lots more skating, crashings, and agonized moanings as body after body fell to the ice. But none of them belonged to Mad Dog.

I guess he was running out of victims, because Krashenburn started shouting, "McDoogle get out here, get out here!"

I couldn't stall any longer. I finished my seventh relacing job and rose unsteadily to my feet.

"Woah, waaa, weeee . . ." my legs wobbled like Jello on a jackhammer until I hit the floor face first. I scrambled to my feet and tried again. "Woah, weeee, waaa . . ."

Repeat performance.

I tried again. This next time I actually managed to get in a step before crashing. (Talk about improvement!) Twenty minutes later I had made it to the edge of the ice, bruised and battered, but ready.

"I see why they call this a violent sport," I said to Arnie.

He just rolled his eyes and turned back to watch
Mad Dog demolish another victim.

K-BAAAMB!

Well, it was now or never. I took a deep breath,
stepped onto the ice, and . . .

Could it be? Was it possible? I didn't fall! It was
a miracle! Somehow I kept my balance. Maybe
everyone was right. Maybe I was good! Maybe I
was a natural! Maybe this was my calling!

"Maybe you should let go of the wall," Arnie
suggested.

I looked down to my hands. I was clinging to the
plexiglass wall for my life. Not a good sign. And
yet, somehow I knew if I could just talk Coach
Krashenburn into building these walls all over the
rink, I had every chance of becoming an Olympic
skating champion.

"Let go," Arnie ordered.

"What?"

"Let go and push yourself off."

"You're crazy!"

He smiled. "*I'm* not the one who wants to play
hockey."

I saw his point.

"McDoogle!" Krashenburn shouted, "Get out
here!" I clinched my eyes shut, said a little prayer,
pushed off, and . . .

Another miracle! I couldn't believe it! I was

skating! I was actually zooming across the ice (if you call creeping forward at about a foot an hour 'zooming'). Then I heard it:

SCRAPE, SCRAPE, SCRAPE, SCRAPE.

I looked up. Mad Dog was racing against Gary the Gorilla for the hockey puck. Considering Mad Dog's pile of unconscious bodies, I should have said a little prayer for Gary. But I decided to pray for myself instead. The reason was simple. The puck was heading directly for me.

I tried to get away—to use my great skating skills and get out of there. Unfortunately, I had no skating skills—except the falling down ones. So that's what I did. With the beauty and grace of a pregnant hippopotamus my feet slid in opposite directions and I crashed.

K-SPLOT!

Unfortunately, this was followed by another sound. A tiny little *clink-plop*. It was the sound of the hockey puck hitting my skates and bouncing up into my lap.

I stared at in horror.

SCRAPE, SCRAPE, SCRAPE, SCRAPE.

I looked up. Gorilla and Mad Dog were barreling toward me. By the glares on their faces it was obvious they had one mission and one mission only. To get that puck. The fact that it was resting on top of a human being named Wally McDoogle made little difference.

SCRAPE! SCRAPE! SCRAPE! SCRAPE!
I felt a sudden wave of sadness. I had always hoped for greater things. Maybe becoming President, or setting the record for the greatest number of consecutive Swirlies. Anything but this. Anything but checking out of life as the world's first and only human hockey puck.

It was time to think quickly. It was time to act swiftly. It was time to sit there and have a good cry. But before my tears fell onto the ice, their bodies crashed into mine.

* * * * *

I don't know how long it took to figure out which leg went to which body, or whose arm belonged to whose chest. Fortunately, I was unconscious during most of the sorting and rearranging. When I did regain consciousness, I wished I hadn't. The ambulance attendants were just putting Mad Dog on the stretcher and carrying him away.

"Sorry, Mad Dog," Coach Krashenburn called. "Maybe next year, after that leg mends, and that concussion heals, and that neck—"

Mad Dog spotted me and growled. "This is all your fault, McDoogle. I'll get you for this, I'll get you real good."

I wanted to apologize, to make some sort of excuse. But it's hard to talk when your heart is beating in your throat. The guy was angry in a serious, maybe-I-should-move-to-Antarctica-to-avoid-him sort of way.

"Don't worry about him," Gary the Gorilla said from beside me. Except for his broken nose and a few more missing teeth, Gary had survived our little run-in pretty well.

"Why shouldn't I worry?" I squeaked.

"He just got out of prison for going crazy and killing a bunch of guys. He wouldn't hurt you."

"Oh," I said. Then turning to him I croaked, "Why not?"

Gary scruntched up his forehead and thought. Finally he shrugged. "Got me."

For some reason I felt no better.

"All right," Coach Krashenburn shouted. "I've seen enough. Hit the showers and I'll have the team roster posted in five minutes."

Everyone hooted and hollered as they skated off. Everyone but me. I just sort of lay there paralyzed for life. Finally one of the guys swung back to give me hand. His name was Cole Dawson.

"Nice check," he grinned as he stooped down to pick me up.

"Thanks," I grimaced.

"You really put Mad Dog out of commission," he said as he twisted my legs around until they faced the right direction. "First time on skates?"

I looked at him. "How did you know?"

"How could I not," he chuckled. "Listen, if you ever want some pointers just let me know." There was something kind about this guy. I liked him immediately.

I wish I could say the same for Coach Krashenburn. "McDoogle," he shouted. "I want to see you in my office."

My heart sank. I knew I hadn't made the team. Not that I wanted to. Believe me, I had enough pain and suffering in my life without looking for more. But still . . . since I could no longer be a writer, and since I had proven I couldn't do anything else . . .

As I limped down to the locker room, I could feel my jealousy starting to churn inside. Opera was the one responsible for all of this. Why didn't he stay where he belonged? Why didn't he stick to his classical music and let me keep to my writing? I had never hated anybody before, but this was sure getting close. Part of me was feeling guilty about that, but most of me was feeling mad . . . real mad.

Krashenburn's office was right next to the locker room. Neither one of my brothers had made the team. A bunch of other guys hadn't either. But for those who did, it was definitely celebration time, in a big way. I looked longingly out the window connecting the coach's office to the locker room and watched the new team members shout and high five. Then Arnie passed out their jerseys and they went ballistic—tearing their clothes, knocking over lockers, ripping up benches. (They were kind of an emotional group.) Of course I wasn't part of that because I was busy listening to the coach as he gazed out the window saying, "You shouldn't feel bad, McDoogle," "There is always next year, McDoogle," and "I hope those guys aren't going to throw that fire extinguisher through my—"

CRASH!

He jumped back as the glass from the window tinkled to the ground and the fire extinguisher rolled to a stop under his desk. Then he cleared his throat and said something that would change my life forever. . . .

"But I do have one position you can fill."

I looked up surprised. "What's that?"

"I don't know if you can handle it. It would mean being in front of thousands of people every game for the entire season."

He definitely had my attention.

"And you must not be afraid of TV cameras or having your picture plastered all over the place."

Most definitely he had my attention.

"And doing lots of guest spots and maybe even movie contracts, and—"

"What is it!" I cried. I tried to sound calm and casual, but it's hard to sound calm and casual when you're standing on top of somebody's desk shouting at the top of your lungs, "What is it! What is it!"

Coach Krashenburn broke into a smile and walked over to his closet. "You would be our mascot, our 'Symbol of Victory.'"

"Symbol of Victory?" I repeated.

With a dramatic flair, Coach Krashenburn threw open the closet door to reveal a giant chicken suit complete with feathered head. A giant chicken suit just big enough for someone my size to fit into.

He proudly held out the suit. "You would become Middletown's most famous and finest feathered friend . . . the one and only . . . magnificent . . . Super Cluck!"

My eyes widened in amazement. Was it possible? Me, famous? Me, our city's *Symbol of Victory*? All right! Just let Opera top that. Just let him try to come close!

"There's only one catch."

"What's that?" I asked as I reached out and stroked the feathers with trembling fingers.

"Super Cluck must have his own identity. No one must ever know you're the one inside. You must always remain anonymous."

My smile dropped faster than a kid's does when

he learns that he's going to summer school. I would become famous, all right. But nobody would know it. How could that be? Isn't that like saying you're rich but penniless?

What type of trick was God playing on me, anyway? It wasn't long before I realized He wasn't playing any tricks—just teaching lessons. . . .

Chapter 5

Heeeeere's Wally

When we last left the marvelously muscular Macho Man McDoogle, he was caught in a time warp that made everything run backwards. It was terrible; people were saying "uoy sselB" before people were sneezing, kids with birthdays were having to rewrap their gifts and hand them back to the givers, and everybody was having to eat their desserts before they ate dinner. (Okay, so every cloud has a silver lining.)

Anyway it was all due to the tyrannical...(insert bad guy music here)... Time Trickster.

With superhuman strength our gigantic good guy shouts, "!pots esaelp ,pots esaelp ,tniop ruoy edam ev'uoy ,thgir lla thgir llA"

"I haven't even begun," the Time Trickster's voice echoes across the universe. "Watch this!"

Before you can say, "Now what?" or is it, "?tahw woN," everything stops running backwards and starts forward again. That's the good news. The bad news is it's going forward at a gazillion.3 miles an hour.

Macho Man leaps off the float, races a half mile to his space craft, the S.S. Musclebound, and closes the hatch...just about the time his mind thinks, *"I think I'll leap off this float."*

That's right dear reader, time is moving faster than our hero can even think.

He turns on the ignition *Err—err—err—err* but nothing happens. He tries again. *Err—err—err—err.* He slams the wheel, thinking, "I knew I should have taken this hunk of junk in for its 4,000,000,000,000,000,000,000,000,000,000 mile checkup. (Actually, at the moment, that's not what he is thinking. At the moment he is thinking, "I think I'll head on over to my spacecraft and climb inside.")

He lets loose a few choice words, "Doggone, tarnation it all, anyway!"

(As a registered good guy he only uses official good-guy vocabulary.) Next he gives the control panel a good, swift kick (something he learned in Spaceship Repair School) and, sure enough, it fires right up.

K-ROARRRRR

He releases the emergency brake, puts on his seatbelt (a must for all role-model types) and drops the ship into "Let's-get-outta-here-fast." It zooms off.

Time is moving faster and faster and faster some more. Kids get through school by 10:30 and college by noon (hmm, another silver lining). Christmas is celebrated every twenty minutes. (Hey, wait a minute, maybe Macho Man should reconsider!)

But it is too late. In 3.4 seconds he lands on Time Trickster's planet and in another 1.2 seconds he finds the fiendish foe's secret laboratory. (Not hard to spot since every wall is covered with every timepiece ever invented...grandfather clocks, sundials, Mickey Mouse watches—even those awful little timers they set when you have to practice the piano twenty minutes a day.)

Once inside the lab, he spots the Time Trickster standing beside his sinister Time Twister Computer. Like all diabolical scientists, Trickster laughs madly as he switches switches, dials dials, and levers levers. Except for the eight or nine extra arms he had attached so he could wear all the latest wristwatches at the same time, he looks like any other notorious nuts-oid.

Looking up, he spots Macho Man and sneers, "So, we meet again, Muscle Mind."

Macho Man nods and says, "I knew I should have taken this hunk of junk in for its 4,000,000,000,000,000,000,000,000,000,000-mile checkup."

Time Trickster grins a twisted grin and suddenly pulls the giant lever of his computer back to "Normal." Everything slows to regular time. Even Macho Man's thoughts catch up.

"Now," Trickster snarls, "you'll be able to fully comprehend the pain and suffering I'm about to inflict."

It is time to act swiftly. Before the terrible Trickster tries any more tricky tricks, our hero leaps to the computer and begins destroying dials, tearing transistors and wrecking readouts. Sparks fly everywhere.

"Oh no!" Time Trickster cries, "Look what you've done!"

"What are you talking about?"

"Oh no!" Time Trickster cries, "Look what you've done!"

"What are you talking about?"

"Oh no!" Time Trickster cries, "Look what you've done!"

And so they go round and round, reliving the same moment again and again. Somehow Macho Man has thrown them into a Time Loop. Will they ever get out? Will they ever escape? Will they ever be able to stop saying...

"Oh no! Look what you've done!"

"What are you talking about?"

And then, just when all appears hopeless, or as boring as another skincare infomercial, Macho Man suddenly—

"Okay everybody, we're here!" called Vice Principal Watkins.

The entire school bus cheered. I looked up from ol' Betsy and frowned. I hated getting interrupted in the middle of writing my superhero stories. I

know I said I'd given up writing, and I had. But
some habits are hard to break. Especially today,
when I was doing everything I could to take my
mind off of Opera. Especially today, when our entire
class was going to sit in the audience of WART-TV's
"Noontime Middletown." With special guest . . .
Opera Livingston!

That's right. The producers of the show thought
it would be cool to interview Opera before he began his week-long job as a TV sportscaster. And
if that wasn't bad enough, Vice Principal Watson
thought it would be even cooler to take us all on
a field trip to watch the noontime show being
broadcast.

Everybody made a big deal out of it . . . everybody but me. I was too busy trying to hold back the
yawns. After all, I was going to be a greater star
than Opera ever imagined. I was going to be
Middletown's "Symbol of Victory."

Of course, I'd be wearing a chicken suit covered
in chicken feathers, and a stupid chicken head.
And, of course, I would never be able to tell any-
one it was me, but that was okay. I kept telling
myself, as long as *I* knew it was me, that was all
that counted. (I kept telling myself that, but unfortunately, I wasn't doing much listening.) The truth
is, I was sick of the way everybody was hanging all
over Opera, especially Melissa Sue Avarice. Talk

about superficial! What anybody can see in her is beyond me.

After we entered the studio, the ushers took us on a backstage tour. They showed us how the living room for "Noontime Middletown" wasn't really a living room a all, but just thin plywood sheets called flats, that were painted and wallpapered to look like a living room. Then, of course, there were all the cameras, the lights, the stagehands running around, and all that other boring stuff.

"Isn't this exciting?" Wall Street whispered as they sat Opera in the guest chair and hooked up a microphone to him.

"Yeah," I yawned again, "if you're into this kind of thing."

"I don't know, Wally," she said. "You've been acting strange all week."

"Me?"

"Yeah. If you ask me, I think you're jealous."

I broke out coughing. "*Me? Jealous?* Don't be ridiculous."

"You never talk to Opera anymore. And every time somebody says something about him you change the subject or act all bored."

Before I could change the subject or act all bored, Sandy Whatabod staggered onto the stage. "Hii thaar boyz 'n girlzz."

I don't want to say the old girl had been drinking,

but it took two stagehands to guide her to her seat and another to keep removing all the little flasks that magically appeared from various pockets and folds in her clothing.

"Okay," the stage manager called out. "We need all you kids to leave the stage and head up to those bleachers for your seats. We're starting in four minutes."

I raised my hand. "Miss, can you tell me where the restroom is?" I really didn't have to go, I just didn't want to be part of the herd. I still wanted to stand out from the crowd, and every little bit helped.

"It's on the other side of the set there," the stage manger pointed, "but hurry."

I nodded and passed behind the set of the make-believe living room. When I got to the window I poked my head inside and saw Opera with some makeup lady hovering over him, giving last minute makeup touches. Disgusting.

I hung out in the bathroom a minute or so, then heard the opening music to the show and decided to get back.

Now please understand that the following was not my fault. . . .

It was *not* my fault that somebody left a big coil of cable just outside the bathroom door.

It was *not* my fault that I stepped into it, got all tangled up, and stumbled into a giant aluminum ladder.

It wasn't even my fault that the ladder went crashing into the back of the nearest flat . . .which tipped forward with a sickening creak. I looked up. *Uh-oh.*

It was like a giant game of slow-motion dominoes. The first flat fell into the second flat, which creaked and fell into the third, which creaked and . . . well, you get the picture.

"She's coming down!" the stage manager screamed.

Everyone scrambled for their lives—cameramen, technicians, Sandy Whatabod, even Opera. Everyone but me. I was still doing my human braiding demonstration as I tried to untangle myself from the cable.

Flats continued falling, props continued crashing, and I continued trying to squirm out of the cable. All this as the music played and the prerecorded announcer said:

"And now, live, it's 'Noontime Middletown'. . . . And here's your host, Sandy Whatabod!"

I finally pulled myself out of the cable and staggered to my feet. Even by my standards the catastrophe was pretty impressive. Everything had fallen. In fact, I was the only thing left standing. Just me and a single camera that happened to be pointed at me with its little red light glowing.

Someone off to the side hissed and waved, but I already knew what was happening. The little red light meant the camera was on, which meant I was standing in front of at least 50,000 viewers. All across the state, people were watching me. Me, Wally-I'm-finally-going-to-be-famous McDoogle.

The person off to the side kept hissing, "Psst, pssst!" But I kept ignoring him. I knew what to do. This was my chance. The big break I deserved. I cleared my throat.

"Pssst, Psssst . . ."

I forced a smile. It was now or never.

"Pssssssst!"

"Hi," I said, "and welcome to our show. My name is Wally McDoogle and I'll be sitting, er, standing in for Sandy this afternoon—"

"Psssssst, Wally!" It sounded like Opera. Obviously he was trying to muscle in on my opportunity. I tried to ignore him.

"In case you're interested, I go to Olympic Heights Middle School and one day plan to be a great—"

"PSSSSSSSSSSST!"

Opera had stepped closer to the camera so I could see him. He was waving wildly, pointing to his pants. I tried to ignore him but he kept pointing. What was his problem? This was *my* moment to shine. But he wouldn't let up. I finally glanced down. Maybe my shirt was untucked, maybe I'd lost a button.

And then I saw it. It wasn't a button. It was my zipper. During all that squirming out of the cable I had somehow managed to unzip my pants—all the way!

So there I was, standing before the whole world, letting everyone know I wore Fruit of the Looms. Yes sir, I had done it. I had finally reached incredible and overwhelming fame. Unfortunately, at that moment, I was wishing for incredible and overwhelming death.

Chapter 6

Opening Night Jitters

The following Monday I got to be just as famous but a lot more dressed. It was the Super Chickens' first game. Actually it was just a practice game, but we had enough crazies on the ice (and in the stands) to make it feel (and hurt) like the real thing.

It was also Opera's first night as a TV sportscaster. He was up in the press booth taking notes for the 11:00 newscast, right along with all the other hot shots.

Down in the locker room my team was getting all worked up. It was typical jock stuff—shouts, punching lockers, eating light bulbs—the usual things to get pumped.

I, on the other hand, sat on the far end of the bench, sneezing my head off.

Ahh-choo!

I had been in my chicken suit a grand total of 2.5 seconds before I had learned a very important fact. I was allergic to chicken feathers.

Ahh-choo!

And by allergic, I'm not talking your typical runny nose or watery eyes. I'm talking about sneezes they name hurricanes after, sneezes that NASA will use to launch their next space shuttle.

AHH-CHOOO!

"McDoogle!" Bruno Pistarini grabbed a towel and wiped off the side of his neck. "If ya don't mind, I'll take my shower afta da game!"

"Sorry," I shrugged. But that was only the beginning of my problems. I soon made another discovery. I turned to Arnie, who had just helped me into my chicken suit. "My arms—*AHH-CHOOO*—where do I put my arms?"

"Chickens don't have arms," Arnie said.

"Yeah, but, *AHH-CHOOO!*"

"Now duck down and let me put this head over you."

"Arnie-*CHOOO!*"

He fought to get the head on. It was way too tight and when he finally got it over my ears, I was afraid it wouldn't come off. There was one other little surprise . . . as soon as he shoved the head on, all the lights went off.

"How's that?" he asked.

"I can't see a thing."

"Just look through the eye opening."

"There is none."

"Sure there is." He poked his hand through the eye hole. Unfortunately he was touching the bottom of my chin. It was six inches too low.

AHH-CHOOO! (ring-ring-ring). The *ahh-choo*ing was another sneeze, the *ring-ring-ring*ing were my ears since the sound had no place to go but straight into my head.

"Tilt your head back," Arnie suggested. "Tilt it way back and look down through the hole."

I did. Farther and farther until at last I saw daylight.

"What do you see?"

"My shoes."

"Perfect."

"But, Arnie, *AHH-CHOOO (ring-ring-ring)*, I can't walk around seeing the tops of my tennis shoes."

"Oh, right," he said, "I'm glad you reminded me." Suddenly he produced a giant pair of chicken feet and started slipping them on me. They were a lot like swim fins only five sizes too big, twice as clumsy, painted bright orange, and *AHH-CHOOO (ring-ring-ring)* covered with chicken feathers.

"Okay men." It was Coach Krashenburn's voice. "Everybody out on the ice! Let's show them what we're made of!"

Everyone shouted and growled as they raced out of the locker room.

"You too, McDoogle—it's time to be a star."

I nodded *AHH-CHOOO (ring-ring-ring)* and headed off. I could hardly wait to make my debut in front of the screaming fans. Although it would have been a little easier if I could walk, move my arms, see, or *AHH-CHOOO (ring-ring-ring)* hear.

* * * * *

It was incredible . . . people screaming at each other, slamming into each other, pounding on each other. And those were just the fans! It was even worse out on the ice. I guess Krashenburn figured what our team lacked in skill we could make up for with an impressive body count. Of course there were a couple nice guys like Cole Dawson. But for the most part, they sat on the bench while monsters like Gary the Gorilla and Bruno Pistarini kept racking up points by racking up players. In no time we earned the reputation of being the meanest and dirtiest team in the league.

It might have bothered me, but I had other things on my mind. As our team's "Symbol of Victory," my job was to whip the crowd into a frenzy of excitement and support. And I succeeded. With my incredible clumsiness I already had them shouting such slogans as, "Get that chicken out of here!" "Our mascot's a moron!" and "Where's Colonel Sanders when we need him?"

Yes sir, I had them eating out of the palm of my wing.

It might have helped if I could see where I was going, or if I could climb the steps without falling ever few feet. Or, when I fell, if I were able to put out my hands to catch myself. But, of course, none of those little luxuries were available. So, whenever I slipped on a step, I would roll and tumble all the way down until I hit the plexiglass wall at the bottom.

BOUNCE, "OUCH, AHH-CHOOO" (ring-ring-ring), BOUNCE, "BOY THAT SMARTS," BOUNCE, BOUNCE, K-RAAASH, "GROAN . . ."

But practice makes perfect. By the third period I was so good at falling, I actually had fans rooting me on—guys with tape measures and felt pens taking bets on how far I'd bounce and roll. Nice fellows and really encouraging. "You can do it, Super Cluck, you can beat your record of 74 steps, I know you can."

I don't remember much toward the end. I do remember lying upside down on my back, staring through the eye hole and seeing the press box at the top of the steps. Inside, I caught a glimpse of good ol' Opera. He was sitting with all the other media bigwigs, scribbling notes for his upcoming broadcast.

Oh, and I remember one other thing. I remember some prehistoric type who smelled like a couple hundred six packs, lifting me over his head and passing me on to the next cave man who passed me on to the next, and so on and so forth.

"Hey guys, *AHH-CHOOO (ring-ring-ring),* put me down, put me down."

"Hey, *HAR-HAR-HAR*—listen to the chicken, he talks."

"Come on guys, *AHH-CHOOO (ring-ring-ring),* chickens aren't supposed to fly."

As if proving my point, every so often someone would accidentally drop me on the floor or onto the sharp edges of seat backs.

Yes sir, it was a lot of fun, but all good things must come to an end and eventually the game buzzer sounded.

I tilted my head back and looked at the scoreboard. We'd won! The score was about a billion to two. It would have been a billion to zero but Bruno got his nets mixed up and scored a couple of points for the wrong side.

As everyone scrambled into the showers, hooting and hollering, Coach Krashenburn shouted,

"You destroyed them! You animals put half their team in the hospital! Way to go!"

More hootings and more hollerings as everyone shouted and high fived. Everyone but Cole Dawson. He just quietly slipped out the door and headed back up to the ice. I didn't see him again until I dragged my aching body out of the locker room to head home.

When I finally got upstairs, there was Cole Dawson out on the ice, all by himself. He had dozens of pucks lined up in a row and was firing one after another into the net over forty feet away. The weird thing was, he didn't miss a single one—every puck landed in the net.

I stopped and watched. The guy was incredible. When he finally finished he looked up and saw me.

"Wow!" I shouted. "That's fantastic!"

He grinned. "Thanks."

"Where did you learn to shoot like that?"

"I've wanted to be a hockey player all my life." He skated toward me. "I started when I was four years old and have never quit."

"How many points did you score tonight?" I asked.

He shook his head. "Coach didn't let me play."

"He didn't?" I couldn't believe my ears.

Cole shook his head.

"But, why not?"

"Krashenburn is of the old school. He thinks the meaner you play, the better you are."

"But . . . but you're better than most of our team put together."

Cole just shrugged.

"Doesn't that make you mad?"

"Yeah," he said, "it makes me mad, real mad. When I see guys like Gary and Bruno getting all the glory, it makes me jealous. But I don't let that jealousy control me. I control it. I use it to help me get better."

"By practicing after games?"

He nodded.

"I tell you, if it were me, I'd tell Coach to fly a kite and just quit."

Cole shook his head. "No. I'm where God wants me. If I stay put, He'll reward me when it's time."

You could have knocked me over with a feather (although I'd prefer it not to be from a chicken). "You believe in God?" I asked.

He nodded. "Yeah. When I gave Him my life, I gave Him the whole thing, including my hockey playing. Even now, when I'm so full of jealousy that I feel like I'm going to explode, I have to let it go and trust that God knows what's best."

I stood with my mouth hanging open. Just switch our names around and you could have been talking about me and Opera. But, unlike Cole, I wasn't letting go of my jealousy. I was hanging onto it with everything I had. I was letting it control me, letting it make me do stupid things . . . like giving up writing to become the world's biggest bouncing chicken.

But, here was Cole, just as angry and just as jealous. Only he was turning it over to God. He was letting God use it to make him a better hockey player. Pretty cool.

"Why don't you grab some skates," he said, "and let me show you some pointers."

"Me?" I squeaked. "I'm not big enough to play hockey. I can't go against those goons."

"Sure you can. Hockey is three things . . . skating, intelligence, and puck handling."

"Not player smashing?"

He grinned. "Not anymore. Coach's style of 'kill or be killed' is really out of date, and it's going to catch up with him one of these days." He tousled my hair. "What say we find you some skates."

We dug up some skates (this time without the pink pom-poms) and soon Cole was teaching me the basics of skating . . . and hockey: "Push and glide, push and glide . . . Stop! Push off! When you take the puck, control it, cradle it . . . and think. Wally, you've always got to think!"

As time went on, he also showed me the difference between . . .

THE WRIST SHOT: "It's accurate and the fastest to get off."
He hit it—*click, pop*—puck into the net.
I hit it—*swish, miss*—stick into the stands.

THE SLAP SHOT: "It's sort of like a golf swing, but you've got to give it all you have!"
He hit it—*crack, whoosh, pop*—puck into the net.
I hit it—*swish, woah! crack*—me onto the ice.

THE BACKHAND SHOT: "Not so popular, but deadly." (Forget the sound effects, let's just say it was more deadly for me than the puck.)

No surprise, but I was awful. I was worse than awful. But Cole stayed right there with me, working away, patiently giving me pointers, and being an all-around good guy.

I was really starting to like him. And the more he worked with me, showing me his hockey stuff, the more I began to wonder if he was right about the jealousy stuff, too. . . . Maybe I should try what he suggested. Maybe I should give it over to God.

Then we were interrupted by those sweet and tender words . . .

"Hey, Moron Mind!" It was my brother Burt. He'd come by to pick me up. "Get the lead out! Your Dork-oid friend's going to be on TV, and we don't want to miss him."

Suddenly I forgot everything Cole had said. Suddenly my jealousy was back in control. And that's too bad. Because if I would have taken Cole's advice I might have had a lot fewer bruises (and smashed body parts) along the way.

Chapter 7

'Fine'

It was 11:22 P.M. Vincent Thrasher looked into the camera and smiled his I'm-an-incredible-hunk-of-a-news-anchorman-and-you-all-know-it smile while saying: "Sitting in for this evening's sportscast, in fact for the entire week, is the winner of our city-wide essay contest. From Olympic Heights Middle School, here's young Opera Livingston. . . ."

"Shh, here he is," Mom said, motioning for all of us to be quiet, "shh, everybody listen now. . . ."

The picture cut to Opera. He said nothing. He just stared back at us wide-eyed, not blinking, not even breathing. I don't want to say the guy froze under pressure, but I've seen Popsicles with more movement.

"So, uh, Opera," Thrasher said, trying to warm him up, "how was your first day as a sports reporter?"

"Fine," Opera answered, still not blinking.
"Uh-huh."

Silence. Thrasher cleared his throat and tried again. "And how was that first assignment covering our Super Chickens?"

"Fine." Still no movement.

"Mm-hmm." Thrasher coughed nervously. "So tonight was their first practice game. How did it go? No, let me guess. . . ."

This time they said it together: "Fine."

Thrasher chuckled uneasily. "Yes, well, uh, um . . . I think we have a clip from tonight's game, why don't we run that?"

"Fine."

The tape began and showed highlights of the game . . . Bruno Pistarini knocking the puck into a goal, Gary the Gorilla knocking the teeth out of a goalie. Gary the Gorilla slapping the puck across the ice, Bruno Pistarini slapping his stick across a face.

"Wow," Vince said, trying to fill in the silence, "those guys really check hard, don't they?" More silence. The scene changed to fans shouting and screaming. "And, hey," he said, "this must be that mascot everyone's talking about."

It was a picture of me in my chicken suit. Of course Mom, Dad, and everybody clapped and cheered. I would have joined them, but that meant moving, and between my bouncing down the steps and the workout Cole had given me, my body was not in the mood.

They showed one of my better falls—a triple, backwards somersault, followed by my usual out of control tumbling and wild bouncing all the way to the bottom and into the plexiglass wall.

"Wow," Vince exclaimed, "that guy must really be an athlete to pull off stunts like that. Pretty impressive, wouldn't you say, Opera?"

"Fine."

Next came a picture of me being passed over the heads of Super Chicken fans.

"Look at his commitment to audience spirit. What do you think of that dedication, Opera?"

"Fine."

The clip was over, and they cut back to Opera still staring. "Well," Vince cleared his throat again, "thanks for that stirring look at sports, Opera, and we'll see you again, tomorrow, right here on WART-TV!"

"Fine."

They cut to a commercial.

Half an hour later I lay in bed. I felt sorry for Opera. Making a total fool of yourself in front of 50,000 viewers is no fun. Believe me I know (although he should count himself lucky that he got to do it with his pants zipped up).

I thought of calling him, of giving him some words of comfort. After all, we used to be best friends. But I couldn't. I figured it served him right. He was only getting what he deserved for stealing my territory. Of course, Cole Dawson's words were also rattling around in my head. *"Turn your jealousy over to God. Trust Him. . . ."* It was quite a tug of war going on inside my brain, until Mom called a cease-fire by knocking on my door and entering.

"Wally, it's Coach Krashenburn. He's on the phone."

I reached for the receiver and answered. "Hello?"

"McDoogle!" He was practically shouting. "The most amazing thing happened. The vice president of RipOff Tennis Shoes was in town and saw us on the news. He wants to do a commercial, a *national* commercial featuring Super Cluck. Isn't that incredible?"

I couldn't believe my ears. "Well, what, what do I do?"

"Just show up at the rink after school tomorrow. Hey, what did I tell ya kid, you're going to be a star!"

I thanked him, hung up, and broke into a grin. Cole Dawson didn't know what he was talking about. I didn't have to hand a thing over to God. Things were already going my way.

Yeah, sure they were.

*   *   *   *   *

"Hey, Wally, did you hear the fantastic news?"

I turned from my school locker to see Wall Street grinning at me. The only thing that could make her smile like that was making money . . . and by the look on her face she'd just won the lottery.

Of course, I was dying to tell her my own news which would be a million times better than hers. Let's face it, next to convincing your little sister she's an outer space alien that has to do all your chores or you'll call the mother ship to take her back, life doesn't get any sweeter than starring in a RipOff Tennis Shoes commercial. Granted, I'd never be able to tell anybody, but in just a few hours I'd be standing in front of the cameras and on my way to super-endorsementhood.

Wall Street continued to beam. "Opera's just agreed to let me be his agent. Isn't that great!"

I shrugged. "Big deal. A week on some local TV station isn't going to make either of you very much—"

She interrupted. "You haven't heard?"

"Heard what?"

"RipOff Tennis Shoes saw his sportscast last night. They want him to be the spokesman for their tennis shoes."

"What?"

"Yeah, they thought it was hilarious the way he kept saying 'Fine,' so they're offering him all sorts of money to say the same thing about their shoes. Our buddy is going to be famous!"

"But . . . but, but, but . . . what about Super Cluck, what about their mascot?"

"Oh yeah, he'll be in the background falling down and stuff, but Opera, *he's* the star, he's the one who gets to do all the speaking! Isn't that fantastic . . . isn't that just . . . 'fine.'" She broke out laughing and headed down the hall repeating the word over and over again. "Fine . . . fine . . . fine." Each time she said it, I knew she heard the sound of bank vaults being opened and money being stacked.

Suddenly there was a commotion at the other end of the hall. I spun around just in time to see Opera appear. He was surrounded by a couple hundred kids. Everybody was laughing and shoving paper at him to autograph. Someone started chanting, "Fine . . . fine . . . fine," and pretty soon everyone joined in. "Fine . . . fine . . . fine."

As he passed, he caught my eye for the briefest second. He looked like he needed some support, but I wasn't about to give him any. No sir. Even now, even after he'd made a total fool of himself last night, he was still upstaging me. I was still having to play second fiddle. Not only that, but I had to fiddle in a chicken suit where no one would even recognize me.

The knots in my stomach grew worse than ever. And then, in my greatest moment of agony, just when I needed tender comfort and understanding the most . . .

"Excuse me?" It was Melissa Sue Avarice. She was flashing her heartbreaking smile and batting her brain-numbing lashes. I glanced over my shoulder to see who she was talking to, but there was nobody there. Just me. Could it be? Was she actually speaking to me? Me, her one and only, *'Wally Dolly?'*

"Hi," I kind of squeaked back.

"It's so good to see you, Willard Dillard." (Hey, with so many admirers, she can't be expected to get every name right.) She held out her autograph book. "I was wondering, would you mind?"

I couldn't believe my ears. How thoughtful, how sweet. "You want me to sign your autograph book?"

Her smile faded. "Of course not. The crowd is so thick I can't get to Opera, but didn't you two used to be friends?"

I looked at her, knowing what was next, but not wanting to believe it. "Yeah . . ."

"So could you, would you mind getting him to sign this for me?" Somehow she managed to bat her eyes, turn up her smile, and hand me her autograph book all at the same time. And, being the man of strength I am, refusing to be manipulated by a pretty face, I held my ground and clearly spoke my mind: "Sure," I squeaked, "how many would you like?"

Chapter 8

Follow the Bouncing Wally

"OKAY EVERYBODY, QUIET PLEASE, QUIET. . . ."

There must have been a hundred movie people all around the ice arena, but when the director called for quiet you could have heard a pin drop.

I stood in the middle of the ice wearing my chicken suit and a pair of RipOff tennis shoes. At one end of the rink were five gigantic Hollywood stunt guys made up to look like hockey players hungry for the kill. At the other end were another five guys equally as big and equally as hungry.

"AND . . . ACTION!"

Both sides raced toward me with everything they had. But I wasn't worried. The special effects people had hooked me up to a bunch of wires which were rigged to a bunch of pulleys in the ceiling. A split second before impact I would jump up in my new RipOff tennis shoes, the special effects guys would yank me into the air, and I'd go sailing off into the stands.

Pretty cool, huh?

Earlier, I'd asked around for Opera, but he was in his private, hotsy-totsy, air-conditioned, dressing room trailer, eating chips to his heart's delight.

"You'll have to wait outside with the rest of his fans if you want to get an autograph," one of the producers told me.

Grrrrr . . .

Now I stood in the center of the rink, watching the stunt men as they bore down on me. They were looking meaner and sounding hungrier by the second.

I waited patiently.

They drew closer.

I waited less patiently.

They drew even closer.

I waited even less—

BAMB!!!

I waited unconsciously.

*   *   *   *   *

Once they revived me and gave me a new chicken suit (I could have also used a new body), we tried again.

"This time," the director explained to his crew, "we need you to pull Super Cluck out just a little sooner, okay guys?"

The special effects team nodded.

"Okay, STAND BY, PLEASE."

They all waited. I prayed.

"AND . . . ACTION!"

The stunt men raced toward me for all they were worth.

I stood there sweating for all I was worth.

Still, I had nothing to fear. After all, these guys were professionals. They wouldn't make the same mistake twice. They were prepared. Too prepared. Just before the two teams turned me into hockey puck paste, the special effects guys yanked my wires. Their timing was perfect.

Unfortunately, their strength wasn't.

In their enthusiasm they pulled way to hard. Suddenly I was rising through the air 10 feet, 20 feet, 50 feet, 75—

K—R A S H ! ! !

That was my head going through the plaster in the ceiling. Fortunately, I was wearing my chicken head which served as a crash helmet, which meant I'd only destroyed half of my brain cells.

When they finally got me down, I could hear Coach Krashenburn getting all over the director's case. "You're too careless! You've got to be more careful!"

"I know, I know," the director agreed.

I smiled. It was nice to have someone sticking up for me.

"You're taking too many risks!" Coach continued to bellow.

"I know, I know . . ."

But Coach wouldn't back off. "I'm down to my last chicken suit—do you know how expensive they are to replace?"

My smile faded.

"I understand," the director said. "And you don't have to worry, because we got the shot."

"You did?"

"That's right. Now we just need one angle of the chicken crashing onto the stairs and bouncing to the bottom, and we're finished."

"All right!" Coach clapped, "glad to hear it!"

I wasn't.

"Okay boys," the director called, "bring out the dummy."

For a moment I thought he was talking about me until I saw them bring out a giant fake chicken. It looked exactly like me—except it didn't have quite as many broken bones.

"We'll drop this stunt dummy from a ladder, let it roll down the steps until it crashes into the bottom wall. Then Mr. Opera will deliver that incredible line of his."

Everyone nodded and somebody ran off to bring in "Mr. Opera." A moment later my ex-buddy, 'Benedict' Opera was escorted onto the set. "Right this way, Mr. Opera. Watch your step, Mr. Opera. Do you need more chips, Mr. Opera?"

With my chicken head off he recognized me instantly.

"Wally?"

"Hey, Opera," I said nervously (we hadn't talked for days). I brushed a chicken feather out of my mouth, "How's it *AHH-CHOOO* going?"

"*You're* Super Cluck?"

"Yeah, that's *AHH-CHOOO* me."

"You're . . . you're incredible!"

I pretended to yawn. "Yeah, so what's your point?" I knew it was a put-down, but it served him right.

He continued to stare. Finally he cleared his throat. "Listen, I uh, know we haven't seen much of each other."

"Oh really," I lied, "I hadn't *AHH-CHOOO* noticed."

That got him good. He tried again. "My schedule's been kinda busy."

"Mine, too."

We stood there facing each other a long moment— me in my chicken suit, him in his three-piece suit.

He tried a third time. "I never got to thank you for giving me the idea on writing about hockey."

"Did I? Hmm, I must have forgotten." Got him again. There was a trace of pain in his eyes. Good. Just as it should be.

Suddenly, one of the assistant directors barged in. "Excuse me, Mr. Opera, we need you to take your position. The stunt chicken's already in place on the ladder and we—"

"What?" I blurted out. "*Stunt* chicken?"

"Well yes, we've brought in a stunt chicken to do the final fall."

"No way," I declared. Pushing the assistant aside, I strode up to the director and said, loud enough for everyone (especially Opera) to hear, "I want to do that fall myself."

"But . . ."

"I've done all the other stunts. I think it's only fair that I finish."

"But there's no need, this stunt chicken is almost as good as—"

"'Almost' is not good enough," I said, sounding more and more like one of the characters in my superhero stories. "Not for me, Wally Super Cluck McDoogle. I want to do the fall myself."

To this day I'm not entirely sure why I volunteered. Maybe it was because I still had three bones that hadn't been broken or a couple of pounds of flesh that hadn't been filleted. Either that or it had something to do with a word. The one that started in *JEAL*, ended with *OUSY*, and didn't have too many letters in between.

In any case, the director looked to Coach Krashenburn. Coach Krashenburn raised his shoulders and shrugged. "It's his body."

After a moment, the director finally turned to his crew. "Okay, everybody. Get rid of the stunt chicken, we're using the real thing!"

"All right," several shouted. A few even clapped. I'd obviously impressed them. That was good. It probably meant they'd all be coming to my funeral.

"Okay, kid," the director said. "Show us your stuff."

I nodded, slipped on my chicken head, *AHH-CHOOO,* and started up the steps. Everyone watched in awe. I could hear them whispering as I passed. For one brief moment I was the hero. Not Opera, but *me.* I was the focus of attention.

I reached the top of the steps and started up the ladder. More silence, more whisperings about my courage and dedication (or ignorance and stupidity, it was hard to hear with the chicken head on). But it made no difference. The point is, Opera may have been the spokesman of this little commercial, but I was becoming its star.

I made it to the top of the ladder.

The director shouted, "*OKAY EVERYBODY, STANDBY!*"

I tensed, waiting to jump, hoping they'd spell my name right in the obituary column.

"*ROLL SOUND!*"

"Speed," somebody shouted.

"*CAMERA!*"

"Rolling," another answered.

"*AND . . . ACTION!*"

I stared down at the steps. It was only a seven foot drop. But it wasn't the drop that worried me. It was the one hundred and fifty three steps between me and that bottom wall. Yet, I'd had more than enough practice the night before, so what did I have to worry about? I was a pro at disaster. One of the best. With that cheery thought running through what was left of my mind, I took a final breath, sneezed, and leaped.

I hit the steps and began the same old bouncing and flying out of control routine . . .

BOUNCE, "OUCH! AHH-CHOOO," BOUNCE, "BOY THAT SMARTS," BOUNCE, BOUNCE.

Faster and faster I rolled. Harder and harder I bounced.

BOUNCE, "OUCH! AHH-CHOOO," BOUNCE, "BOY THAT SMARTS EVEN MORE," BOUNCE, BOUNCE.

Everything was a blur of spinning lights, grinning crew members, and super-hard concrete steps, lots and lots of super-hard concrete steps. The pain was so great I was about to pass out, but I hung on. I had to make this look as good as possible. Finally I hit the last step and smashed into the wall:

K-RAAASH, "GROAN . . ."

And then, directly in front of the camera, I heard Opera say the magical word: "Fine."

"CUT!" the director yelled. "That was beautiful. Perfect!" Everyone clapped and cheered. And then, as they were helping me to my feet, I heard him shout. "That was such a good fall, I want to get a a lot more angles, then go in for five or six close-ups. We should be through by midnight. I tell you Super Cluck, you were magic."

I really wanted to thank him, but it's hard to talk when you don't have any teeth left in your mouth.

* * * * *

When we last left the muscular Macho Man, he had just destroyed Time Trickster's computer. Now they are caught in a Time Loop, doomed forever to say:

"Oh no! Look what you've done!"

"What are you talking about?"

But, not wanting to be the only McDoogle superhero who doesn't save the day, Macho Man muscles up all of his muscles, brings his bulging biceps down hard onto the computer, and destroys the Time Loop and the computer. Unfortunately, that's not the only thing he's destroyed.

Sparks spark, smoke smokes, and electricity electrifies. Suddenly, all lights go out.

"Forget to pay your electric bill?" Macho Man shouts.

"No, you ninny!" Time Trickster screams. "You've destroyed it."

"Destroyed what?"

"Time."

"What about it?"

"You've destroyed it."

"Destroyed what?"

"Time."

"What about it. Listen, are we stuck in that time loop thing again?"

"No BB brain," the Trickster shouts, "You've destroyed time!"

Macho Man scoffs. "I don't have time for this nonsense."

"Precisely. You don't have time, because there is no time. You've destroyed it."

"Wait a minute!"

"There are no minutes."

"Just give me a second."

"There are no seconds."

Macho Man slaps his head in disbelief. "Wow. I really blew it this time, didn't I?"

"No, you didn't."

"Why not?"

"Because there is no 'this time' to have blown it in."

Macho Man gives a heavy sigh. All this double talk is giving his brain whiplash. "Can't you fix your Time Twister and bring time back?"

"No way."

"Why not?"

"Because I haven't got the time."

"My head is hurting."

"It's about time."

"What is?"

"Your headache."

"Knock it off!"

"I'd love to, but I——"

"I know, I know," Macho Man groans, "but you haven't got the time."

"You're catching on."

"So what do we do now?"

"There is no 'now' to do anything in."

"We're stuck like this forever?"

"There is no 'forever'."

"I'm going to punch you."

"You can't punch me," Time Trickster cries, "because you——"

"I know, I know, 'I haven't got the time.'"

"You've got it now."

"No, I haven't."

"That's right."

And then, just before Macho Man's mind is permanently muddled, there is a sudden——

"Wally?—Wally?" It was Mom calling up the stairs. "Are you in bed yet?"

"Just about," I shouted.

"Well, hurry up. Tomorrow night's your first official game. You want to be good and rested for it."

"All right, all right." Reluctantly, I shut down ol' Betsy and crawled into bed. The commercial had taken all day to make. I'm not sure which hurt more, my body or my pride. It was probably a tossup.

Like Macho Man, I was totally trapped. Every time I tried to outshine Opera, things got worse. I had done everything—well, almost everything. There was still Cole Dawson's way, turning my jealousy over to God.

I shook my head. No, I was going to outshine Opera on my own, even if it killed me. (So far it was doing a pretty good imitation.)

There was still tomorrow night, the first official game of the season. Maybe I could pull off something then.

Chapter 9

Let the Game Begin

School was worse than ever. Everybody and their brothers (and sisters . . . and probably a few aunts, uncles, and cousins) were talking about Opera's incredible commercial. Of course, I wanted to tell them about his incredible co-star, but couldn't. Super Cluck's identity had to remain a secret.

Then, just when it couldn't get any worse, it did. WART-TV decided it would be cool to have my ex-buddy cover Middletown's very first hockey game . . . live. He would help their regular sports reporter run a play-by-play commentary. I groaned at the news. What was next, a parade in his honor, a holiday on his birthday?

I'd soon find out . . .

That evening, down in the locker room, the players were getting pumped up to play the

Slattervile Mongooses. I don't want to say Coach Krashenburn was turning our guys into animals, but if you've ever heard the zoo around feeding time, you'd get a pretty good picture of what was going on.

"All right, men," he said, "this is the first official game for the Super Chickens!"

"ROAR" . . . "BARK, BARK, BARK" . . . "HOWL" . . . "OO-OO-AH-AH-EE-EE" . . . *"CLUCK, CLUCK, AHH-CHOO"* (that last, of course was me).

"I want you to get out there and give it everything you've got!"

"ROAR" . . . "BARK, BARK, BARK" . . . "HOWL" . . . "OO-OO-AH-AH-EE-EE."

"Oh, and one other thing. Mad Dog Miller is back."

"ALL RIGHT!" . . . *"ROAR"* . . . *"BARK, BARK, BARK"* . . . *"HOWL."*

"But he's playing for the other team."

"meow" . . . *"whimper, whimper, whimper"* . . . *"whine"* . . . *"uh-oh."*

"Come on, men, you can do it. He's just one guy."

"Yeah, but . . . I don't think I can play with this hangnail . . . is that my mommy calling?"

A minute later we were trudging up the stairs. Everyone was scared spitless (or in their case droolless). Everyone remembered the tryouts and how Mad Dog had piled up the bodies of anybody who got in his way. Then, of course, there was his little threat against my life. What had he said, "I'll get you for this, McDoogle—I'll get you real good?"

Oh boy . . .

"Hey, Wally?" I tilted back my chicken head to see Cole Dawson at my side.

"Hi, *Ahh-chooo,* Cole."

"I just want to make sure you're okay," he said. "I mean with Mad Dog's threat on your life and everything."

I grinned. "Got it covered. I'm going to be nice and safe up there in the stands. All I have to do is bounce down steps and be tossed, mauled, and stomped on by a thousand crazed fans. You're the one in danger, out there on the ice with him."

Cole nodded. "Only if Coach lets me play."

"Oh, yeah, I forgot about that."

"Hey, did you hear the news?"

"What's *Ahh-choo* that?"

"Some guy from NBC Sports is up in the announcer's booth."

"Here?"

"Yeah, I guess he's checking out your buddy, Opera—to see if they might use him for the next Olympics. You know, a kid's point of view thing. Pretty cool, huh?"

My heart dropped. In fact, if it sank any lower, they'd have to dig a ditch for me to drag it through.

Come on. Enough was enough. Was there no end to my humiliation?

Not yet . . .

The game finally got underway. The face-off between Gary the Gorilla and Mad Dog was pretty good—except for the part where they carried Gary off on the stretcher. But that's okay, we had fourteen other guys. Until the next face-off. Then we had thirteen.

"Hey, Krashenburn!" the Mongooses' coach shouted. "How's it feel, getting a taste of your own medicine? You wanna play dirty, we'll play dirty!" Then, turning to his star player he shouted, "Sick 'em, Mad Dog, go get 'em boy!"

Mad Dog growled and continued his mission of seek and destroy.

I would love to tell you about the rest of the game, but the fans in the stands had all seen me on the news and they were expecting some action. So, not wanting to disappoint, I started walking up those familiar steps and in no time flat was up to (or is it down to) my usual crash and burn routine. Just like old times:

BOUNCE, "OUCH, AHH-CHOOO," BOUNCE, "BOY THAT SMARTS," BOUNCE, BOUNCE, K-RAAASH . . . "GROAN."

A couple of times I glanced up to the press booth and saw Opera yacking away at the camera. And

Mr. Hot Shot, NBC Sports Guy was right there watching his every move. I got real angry and threw myself down the stairs even harder. (Not only is jealousy painful, but it makes you pretty stupid, too.)

The score was close during the first two periods. We'd pull ahead by one or two goals, then Mad Dog would destroy one or two of our players. It seemed a pretty fair trade-off. But by the time we headed into the locker room after the second period, the score was tied and Coach was looking a little worried. Something about having only eight players left made him nervous.

Of course, Mad Dog would serve some time in the penalty box, but to Mad Dog it seemed a small price for the overwhelming joy the destruction brought him.

"Okay, men, look alive. (Not an unreasonable request, except for those who had already run into Mad Dog.)

"Dawson?" Coach turned to my buddy, Cole. "If worse comes to worse, I'll have to put you in, so get ready."

"Yes sir." Cole beamed.

"And don't try any of that fancy skating stuff. We play the old fashion hockey of hit or be hit. Kill or be killed." The phrase must have sparked a memory in Krashenburn's mind, because he suddenly turned to me. "McDoogle?"

"*Ah-choo?*"

He handed me a jersey. "Slip this over your chicken suit. I want you to sit on the bench with the rest of the team."

I couldn't believe my ears. "Me?"

"That's right."

"I don't have to go up into those stands any more?"

He nodded.

My pulse quickened, my stomach flipped, my heart flew.

"I put your name on the roster so I can use you as a back up in case Mad Dog destroys all our other players."

My pulse stopped, my stomach wretched, my heart crashed.

"Me?" I repeated, this time clucking and trying to flap my wings. I hoped he'd get the hint, but he'd already turned back to the rest of the team.

"Okay, men, I don't have to tell you what this game means to us, so let's get out there and show them what we've got . . . or at least what we've got left."

It was a pathetic sight, seeing everybody sniffle and whine as they crawled up the stairs. Everybody but Cole Dawson, who was looking forward to finally playing . . . and me, who wasn't looking forward to finally dying.

* * * * *

The score was 4 to 4. It was kinda cool sitting down at ice level watching the whole thing. Bruno Pistarini won the face-off and our guys skated up a storm—most of the time just to stay out of Mad Dog's way.

Our forwards got the puck and moved it down the ice.

The arena announcer was up in the booth bellowing through the loud speakers: "And the Super Chickens have the puck . . ."

I threw a look over my shoulder and saw Opera in the booth, too. He caught my eye and gave a little wave. I was too cool to wave back. After all, he was just a TV commentator. I was an official player.

"Cradle it," Coach Krashenburn was yelling. "Cradle it!"

They passed it back and forth, working it, looking for a shot.

And then, with a quick fake, Bruno, who was playing left wing, slipped past his man and started for the goal. The crowd cheered. Bruno deked once, then fired an incredible backhand. It was a beautiful shot, but not as beautiful as their goalie's save. Their guy barely got his stick on it, but barely was enough. He deflected the puck to the right corner.

"Dig it out of there!" Coach shouted. "Dig it out!"

They dug . . . until Mad Dog arrived. Then they scattered . . . for their lives.

"Defense!" Krashenburn screamed. "Defense!"

And so it went back and forth. Offense, defense. Defense, offense. And still the score stayed the same. From all the time he had spent in the hospital, it was obvious Mad Dog was out of shape and running out of steam. A whole half period passed and he didn't destroyed a single one of our guys. Maybe there was hope, maybe we'd pull a goal off yet, maybe I still believed in the tooth fairy.

With five minutes to go, Mad Dog raced down the ice past our bench and suddenly scraped to a halt. The game was still going on, but something *or someone* had caught his eye.

Uh-oh.

I ducked my head, pretending to adjust my laces, hoping he wouldn't notice me. No such luck. Suddenly I smelled the most vile and hideous smell imaginable. It was so bad I thought my sister had got a job cooking at the concession stand. Then I realized it wasn't my sister's cooking, it was someone's breath. Slowly, I lifted my head. There was Mad Dog, leering over the wall, glaring into my face. "I haven't forgotten, McDoogle," he growled. "You're still on my list!"

I opened my mouth. It was time to make peace, time to smooth his feathers. Unfortunately it wasn't *his* feathers that were the problem. I looked him squarely in the eyes and suddenly *AHH-CHOO*ed all over his face.

He lunged at me, but I leaped back. "You wouldn't hit a kid with glasses, would you?"

He snarled.

I guess I had my answer. Spotting my chicken head, I reached over, grabbed it, and yanked it hard over my face, too hard. "You wouldn't hit a chicken with glasses?"

"No," he growled, wiping his face. "If it was a chicken, I'd ring its neck, pluck its feathers, and eat it raw."

Suddenly Coach Krashenburn stepped in. "Come on, Mad Dog. McDoogle's one of my players, now. Leave him alone."

Mad Dog looked shocked. "Him? A player?"

"Yeah."

Mad Dog stared blankly. (Now, for any thought to come into Mad Dog's mind was a special occasion. But for the one that was currently forming, they should have held a national holiday.) He slowly turned to Krashenburn. "Where's the rest of your team?"

"You're looking at them," Krashenburn said. "Dawson and McDoogle are the only ones I got left."

Mad Dog broke into a menacing grin that bared his teeth (actually there were more gums than teeth). He spun back to the game and counted our six players on the ice. He turned back to Cole and me and counted two players. Being the math wiz he is, it only took three or four minutes to realize how many of our players he'd have to destroy to get me out on the ice.

He began to chuckle, then to laugh, then to howl.

I began to pray.

He rejoined the game with new strength and energy. In 3.2 seconds he wiped out Bruno Pistarini. The way Mad Dog dropped low, checked Bruno, and sent him hurtling into the boards, it was a work of art. Poetry in pulverizing motion.

It was time for another replacement. Coach Krashenburn turned to Cole. "Okay, Dawson, get out there!"

Cole grinned as he pulled on his helmet and hopped over the wall. This was his big moment.

The announcer shouted into the mic "And in for the Super Chickens is number 34, Cole Dawson."

The Mongooses had the puck and worked it down the ice. As fast as they were, Cole was faster. He wasn't interested in hard checking anybody or being some sort of a mauler. He was only interested in getting that puck. And that was his secret. It was incredible to watch his speed. I'd never seen anybody with such quick recovery and reflexes.

Neither had the crowd. They started rising to their feet.

"What's that guy's name?" somebody shouted.

I turned around. I was still wearing my chicken head. In fact I had yanked it on so hard, I figured I'd being wearing it though college graduation. But I managed to lean back and shout through the opening, "Dawson! His name is Cole Dawson!"

There was a loud cheer. I turned to see Cole stealing the puck and moving up the ice. Soon the crowd began to chant, "Daw-son, Daw-son, Daw-son!"

This only fired Cole up more as he passed the puck back and forth to his teammates.

I threw a look to Krashenburn. His mouth hung open.

The crowd grew louder: *"DAW-SON, DAW-SON, DAW-SON!"*

The way Cole kept outmaneuvering his man, he could have made four or five shots. But he was waiting for that perfect one. And then, just as our center screened the goalie's vision, Cole reached back for a slapshot, swung his stick and—

P O W !

Unfortunately the *POW* wasn't the puck being hit. It was Cole's body being hit . . . by Mad Dog, who'd just come out of the penalty box. As an obvious cross-checking foul, it had the crowd up and booing. But the ref didn't see a thing. Maybe he did. Or maybe the fact that the ref and both linesmen were now wearing Mongoose T-shirts somehow affected his judgment.

Cole made it back to his feet, but the Mongooses had recovered the puck and tore down the ice. Then, with less than a minute on the clock, they fired a sloppy slapshot.

Our goalie dropped out of the crease to easily bat it away, except for Mad Dog who batted *him* away . . . at about 300 miles per hour. The puck hit the net, the goal siren sounded, and the paramedics rushed in.

It took ten minutes to dig our goalie out of the ice . . . which was just long enough for Krashenburn to start strapping pads and gloves all over my body.

"Coach . . . what are you doing?"

"These are goalie knee pads, McDoogle."

"But . . ."

"These are goalie gloves."

"But . . .but . . ."

"And this is a goalie face mask."

He tried to pull off my chicken head, but it wouldn't budge. So he finally just threw the face guard over the top.

"What am I supposed to do, Coach? Tell me! Tell me!"

"Try not to get killed."

Chapter 10

Super Cluck to the Rescue

I eased out onto the ice, praying to God all the way. I wasn't picky about His answer. I didn't care if it was an earthquake, hurricane, or just your above-average, giant meteorite smashing into the arena and wiping us all out. Anything would do, just as long as it struck before Mad Dog did.

Once again the announcer's voice echoed: "In as a replacement goalie for the Super Chickens . . . Wally McDoogle."

The crowd cheered me on with a resounding . . . "Who? What's that punk doing out there? Who's the idiot wearing the chicken head!"

Cole joined my side. "Can't you get that thing off?" he asked as he tugged at the head.

"It's stuck," I shouted as we skated toward our goal. "Cole, what do I do? I don't know a thing about playing goalie!"

"The concept is simple," he said. "Just get hit by whatever flies in your direction."

"No sweat," I said, suddenly feeling better. "I do that all the time at school."

He grinned. "We've got fifty-two seconds left. I'll try to keep the puck down at the other end and run the clock out so it never gets up to you. I'll save my shot until the very last second."

"Thanks," I said as I took my position squarely in front of the net. Everything was set. Well, almost everything.

"Wally!" Cole shouted.

"Yeah?"

"You've got to turn around, you've got to face the game."

"Thanks!" As I turned around, I couldn't help throwing another look up to Opera in the booth. Like everyone else, he was standing and staring at me in amazement. Great, I thought. I may die, but at least I'll die with the recognition I deserve.

There was a loud crack as the ref threw down the puck. There were lots of sticks slapping until Cole finally got the face off.

I looked at the clock:

47 Seconds

Cole moved up the ice, passing it back and forth to the other players. A couple of times he could have broken for the net. But he didn't. And I knew

why. He was going to wait 'til the last possible
second so they couldn't come my way.

35 Seconds

The crowd was on its feet chanting: *"DAW-SON,*
DAW-SON, DAW-SON." And still he waited—
cradling the puck, passing it to a teammate, receiv-
ing it again, and waiting for that perfect moment.

29 Seconds

But Mad Dog had had enough. He spun out of
position, left his man unchecked, and raced at
Cole from behind.

"Look out!" I shouted, "Cole, look out!"

But there was too much noise for him to hear.
He caught movement out of the corner of his eye
and turned. He was too late. Mad Dog checked
him with everything he had. Cole smashed into
the wall as if he were shot from a cannon. There
would have been less damage if he had been.

"COLE!!!" I wanted to get down there to see him,
but I knew I couldn't leave my position.

Our trainer raced out. After a couple of minutes
he lifted Cole to his feet and carefully helped him
off the ice.

The crowd began giving him a standing ovation.
Even though Cole was in pain, he managed to
smile and give them a half-wave. And for good
reason: He had finally proven his point. By refusing to give in to Coach's methods, and waiting for

God to have His way, Cole had become the hero. He would be back. Maybe not for this game, but for others. And when that happened, he would return as the Super Chickens' star player.

Unfortunately, that didn't help me much. I looked at the clock:

22 Seconds

The Mongooses got the puck and wasted no time. They headed straight for me!

"Let me have it!" Mad Dog shouted, "Let me have it, I want to destroy him. Let me have it!"

They fired him the puck. There was no missing the look of joy in Mad Dog's eyes as he drove the black disk across the blue line and directly toward me. He had wiped out all of his other buddies—Gary the Gorilla, Bruno Pistarini, Cole Dawson . . . now there was only one left. His favorite . . .

Dead Meat McDoogle.

I stood there frozen, unable to move. I didn't know a thing about playing goalie . . . much less surviving a puck that would be traveling through my chest at the speed of sound. My entire life flashed before my eyes. Well not all of it. Mostly just the part about why I was standing here. No matter how you looked at it, it all came down to one word: *Jealousy*. That was it, painfully plain and stupidly simple.

But instead of giving it over to God like Cole had

done, I had hung on to it, letting it turn me into the world's biggest sitting duck, er, chicken. I don't remember exactly what I prayed, but I do remember asking for another chance to do it the right way . . . and maybe even squeezing in some goalie lessons for the next time.

Then I heard a voice:

"Move around the crease!"

I looked up, surprised. Where was the voice coming from?

"Move around that blue half circle in front of you." It was Opera. He had grabbed the PA microphone from the arena announcer and was shouting into it. "Keep moving, Wally, don't stop!"

I couldn't believe my ears. Neither could anybody else.

Everyone looked up to the press booth to see Opera clinging to the PA microphone and giving me instructions. I guessed this wasn't normal procedure by the way the announcer and everybody kept swearing and trying to grab the mic from him.

But Opera would not give in. He was going to help me and nothing would get in his way.

What a guy.

I looked to Mad Dog.

What a monster.

He was practically on top of me.

"Watch the fakes!" Opera's voice echoed through the speakers. "He'll deke twice and shoot on the third, he always does."

I nodded and prepared myself. If Opera was sacrificing his career as a sports reporter to save me, the least I could do was to stay alive long enough to see if he succeeded.

Mad Dog was fifteen feet away . . . then ten.

I kept moving in front of the net just like Opera said.

Mad Dog pretended like he was going to shoot it forehand, then he switched to his backhand. But I wasn't fooled. Opera had said two dekes, so I held my ground.

He went back to his forehand. This was it.

He hit the puck.

I leaped in its direction. At the last second I closed my eyes, and:

SMASH . . . RATTLE, RATTLE, RATTLE!

Smash . . . rattle, rattle, rattle? What's a *Smash . . . rattle, rattle, rattle?* I was expecting a *K-Bamb!* you're dead, or a *Rip!* now you have a hockey puck hole through your chest. But a *Smash . . . rattle, rattle, rattle?*

I looked around dazed. Where had it gone? Where was the puck? I turned to the audience. Everyone was shouting and pointing to the top of my head. What did they mean? The only thing on the top of my head was another head, the giant chicken one.

They kept motioning and yelling until I finally understood their words: "Your beak!" they shouted. "It's in your beak!"

I reached up and ran my hand inside the beak. At last I felt something. The hockey puck! I had caught the hockey puck in my beak! What luck!

I looked to the clock:

12 Seconds

Now what?

"Drop it on the ice!" It was Opera again. I looked up to the announcer booth. Opera had built a barricade of chairs to keep the other reporters and announcer away. If there was ever any doubt that he had totally destroyed his career as a reporter it was over now. Opera was history. But he didn't care. "Drop the puck down," he shouted. "You've got 12 seconds. Skate the puck out and let it drop down."

I stared at him, not believing. Was that sort of thing legal?

"Hurry!"

With nothing to lose (but my life) I jerked my head down. The puck rolled out of my beak and fell to the ice. Everyone stared at it dumbfounded. No one was moving. Which explained Opera's next command. "GO FOR THE GOAL!" he shouted. "GO, WALLY, GO!"

I guess he figured since I was the only one not paralyzed with complete amazement I was the only one able to make the move. While the players and ref stared in disbelief, I pushed the puck ahead of them with my stick and started forward.

The crowd picked up Opera's words and started to chant: *"GO, WALLY, GO! GO, WALLY, GO!"*

I glanced up at the clock:

10 Seconds

"GO WALLY, GO! GO WALLY, GO!"

I was doing my best, but it's hard to "go" when you can barely stand, let alone skate. Still, I remembered some of Cole's pointers, and made progress.

08 Seconds

By now the ref and players had regained a certain amount of consciousness. No one had blown a whistle, so I guess they figured it was all legal. Everyone began pursuit. I could hear their skates clacking and scraping behind me. And I could hear growling and howling. Growling and howling that could only belong to one very mad, Mad Dog Miller.

"GO, WALLY, GO!" the crowd continued to chant.

I crossed the blue line. Up ahead of me their goalie looked pretty confused. Behind me I could hear the thundering of skates and howling that pierced the air. Mad Dog had nearly caught up.

I pushed off one more time, two more times.

"DUCK DOWN!" Opera shouted. "DUCK!"

I forgot the puck and dropped into a tight little ball. Just in time. I was hit by a thousand pounds of very angry revenge. A thousand pounds whose force was so powerful that it sent both of us smashing onto the ice and sliding forward, completely out of control.

I don't know how long we slid, but I managed to get a peek at a very frightened goalie scrambling out of our way. And for good reason . . . we were heading directly for his net!

"THE PUCK!" Opera shouted. "HIT THE PUCK WITH YOUR STICK OR IT WON'T COUNT!"

I looked all around. The only puck he could be talking about was the one directly under my chin. I wasn't sure what the big deal was, but he hadn't been wrong, yet. I worked my stick up to my chin and gave the puck a little tap with it. Now it was zooming down the ice just inches ahead of my face.

And then we hit:

K-BAMB KRASH!!!
BUZZZZZZZ
RRRRRRRRRRRRR

The *K-BAMB KRASH* was Mad Dog and me hitting the net so hard that we broke it loose and smashed with it into the wall.

The *BUZZZZ* was the end of the game buzzer.

But it was the *RRRRRRR* that threw me. Why

was the score siren going? Then I looked down and saw that I was lying beside the hockey puck. The very puck that had crossed the goal line just ahead of us to score the winning point.

Of course, everyone was going ballistic—crazed fans, screaming players, whimpering Mad Dogs. But what I remembered most, was one lone kid's voice shouting through the PA system:

"THAT A BOY, WALLY—YOU DID IT! THAT'S MY BEST FRIEND, EVERYBODY! THAT'S WALLY McDOOGLE!"

Chapter 11

Wrapping Up

The next few weeks were kind of boring. Of course there were the usual doctors, hospital beds, and casts over every part of my body. But that was nothing new for someone with my experience in pain and mayhem.

Cole called a few days later. It was pretty cool. Coach Krashenburn promised that as soon as Cole recovered from his injuries, he would put him in the starting lineup. He had to. With all the fan mail Cole was getting, Krashenburn didn't have a choice.

Wall Street swung by a couple of times. "I'm selling your life story to the movies, but I'm stuck on a title. Right now it's between *Wally McDoogle: Klutzy Cluck* and *Molting McDoogle: Heroic Hen*."

I said both were nice but that she was somehow missing the hockey angle. She agreed and said she'd come back tomorrow.

The next day she showed up with an even better idea. "What say we open up a restaurant. We could call it 'Chickenpucks.'"

"Chickenpucks?"

"Yeah. We could sell Chickenpuck Burgers—fried chicken formed to look like hockey pucks."

"I don't think—"

"Sure, and we dip them in creamy dark chocolate so they're almost the color of hockey pucks, then we smear just a little ketchup on top to look like your blood, then add a few feath—"

"Sounds great," Opera said as he strolled into the room, munching on a bag of chips, "when do we eat?"

Wall Street glanced first to me, then to Opera. She knew we had unfinished business, so she made some excuse to leave. "I've got to get the Chickenpuck recipe patented before someone steals it," she said.

"I wouldn't worry," I mumbled, but she didn't hear.

Now it was just Opera and me. I hadn't seen the guy since the game. I knew I had a lot of thanking to do, and by the way I'd been treating him, even more apologizing. In fact, I was wondering how he'd ever forgive me for being such a jerk.

But how do you put all of that stuff into words?

"Opera . . ."

"Yeah, Wally?"

"Listen, um, uh . . . I've really learned a lot about jealousy lately and, uh . . ."

Suddenly Opera reached into his knapsack and pulled out a bag of his prized Super-Duper, Double-Fried Salties—the chips he keeps in his bank safe-deposit box.

"Well, what I'm trying to say is, I really learned my lesson and, uh . . ."

Without a word, Opera opened the bag, took a moment to savor the heavenly aroma, then offered the first chip to me. Gratefully, I took one, and munched away—secretly hoping I wouldn't break a tooth on their super-duper crunchiness.

He reached in the bag and started eating, too.

I cleared my throat. "Okay, what I'm trying to say is I'm really sorr—"

"Have another?" He held the bag out to me. I looked at him a moment. Slowly I started to understand. This was how he wanted to make up. This was how he said everything was okay—the two of us just sitting in silence, eating the most valuable potato chips in the world.

I nodded a thanks, and reached in for another. So did he.

And there we sat, munching away. We never brought up the subject again. It was like we both already knew, and nothing more ever needed to be said.

When we finished off the bag, Opera rose to his feet.

"See ya tomorrow," he said.

"Yeah," I said, "See ya."

I leaned back on my pillow and sighed. Not only had I learned a valuable lesson about jealousy, but I had just made peace with my best friend while putting down about ten thousand salt-saturated calories. Life was good. Everything was good. Well, everything except Macho Man's little predicament.

Reaching for ol' Betsy, I snapped her on and finished my story. . . .

When we last left Macho Man, he and the entire universe were in the dark. He had just killed Trickster's tweaked-out Time Twister Computer. Unfortunately that also meant killing time...literally. Every form of time was dead—dinner*time*, pas*time*, show*time*, bed*time*. (Wait a minute, was that another silver lining?) In any case, something has to be done. And since we only have three pages left of this story, he better work fast!

Time Trickster's mind works like clockwork—okay, so we can't use CLOCK-work—How 'bout homework? Housework?

"We have to use our brains!" Time Trickster shouts. "We have to sneak up and catch it."

"Catch what?"

"Time."

"How?"

"Hit me on the head."

"That's stupid."

"That's why I'm asking *you* to do it. Just hit me on the head, and I'll explain."

Macho Man tries to think it through, but since thinking has never been one of his strong suits, he shrugs his stupendously strong shoulders, bulges his brawny biceps, and barely taps the bad guy on the bean—which sends Trickster staggering and falling into a fit of unconsciousness.

"Sorry," Macho Man says as he finally revives Trickster. "I guess I don't know my own strength."

"That's okay, Miniature Mind. I want you to do it again, just like that last *time.*"

"But there is no last ti—"

"Shhh," the Trickster whispers. "If you do it again, just like the last *time,* we'll prove there was a last *time.* And if we prove there was a last *time,* then we can prove there is time. Got it?"

"Got it," Macho Man nods, not getting it at all.

"Good." Trickster braces himself. "Okay, hit me exactly as you did before."

Macho Man leans back and carefully crashes the Trickster's cranium. Repeat performance of the staggering and falling routine. Only this time, as Trickster's lights go out, the universe's lights come on.

"We did it!" Macho Man shouts. "We brought back time."

"That's terrific," Time Trickster mumbles as he comes to, and rubs another lump on his head.

"Well, I hope you've learned your lesson," Muscle Man says as he helps Trickster to his feet.

"I sure have. I've learned that above all else..." he pauses and looks at Macho Man with a twinkle in his eye... "I've learned that TIME doesn't pay." Trickster busts a gut laughing.

It is the worst joke Macho Man has ever heard, but he tries to smile politely. Suddenly, Trickster throws his arm

around him and fires off another groaner.
"I tell you, Mutant Mind, I really didn't
mind killing time, after all...time's
killing me." Again he laughs.

Macho Man fidgets nervously. As they
turn for the expected stroll off into
the sunset, he wonders if maybe he hit
Trickster just a little too hard on the
noggin.

"Say Macho Man, what time is it when
an elephant sits on your fence?"

Now he's sure of it.

But, turning the Time Trickster into
the world's worst comic seems a small
price to pay. After all, time is once
again safe and secure. Once again time
is absolutely predictable and depend-
able. (Now if he could just get his hands
on those guys who keep changing us back
and forth to Daylight Savings Time.) In
any case, it has been another victori-
ous victory of another adventuresome
adventure with the marvelously muscular and oh so manly...(insert superhero
music here)...Macho Man McDoogle!

By the way, what is the purpose of
Daylight Savings Time?

You'll want to read them all.

THE INCREDIBLE WORLDS OF WALLY McDOOGLE

#1—My Life As a Smashed Burrito with Extra Hot Sauce

Twelve-year-old Wally—"The walking disaster area"—is forced to stand up to Camp Wahkah Wahkah's number one all-American bad guy. One hilarious mishap follows another until, fighting together for their very lives, Wally learns the need for even his worst enemy to receive Jesus Christ. (ISBN 0–8499–3402–8)

#2—My Life As Alien Monster Bait

"Hollyweird" comes to Middletown! Wally's a superstar! A movie company has chosen our hero to be eaten by their mechanical "Mutant from Mars!" It's a close race as to which will consume Wally first—the disaster-plagued special effects "monster" or his own out-of-control pride . . . until he learns the cost of true friendship and of God's command for humility. (ISBN 0–8499–3403–6)

#3—My Life As a Broken Bungee Cord

A hot-air balloon race! What could be more fun? Then again, we're talking about Wally McDoogle, the "Human Catastrophe." Calamity builds on calamity until, with his life on the line, Wally learns what it means to FULLY put his trust in God. (ISBN 0–8499–3404–4)

#4—My Life As Crocodile Junk Food

Wally visits missionary friends in the South American rain forest. Here he stumbles onto a whole new set of impossible predicaments . . . until he understands the need and joy of sharing Jesus Christ with others. (ISBN 0–8499–3405–2)

#5—My Life As Dinosaur Dental Floss

It starts with a practical joke that snowballs into near disaster. Risking his life to protect his country, Wally is pursued by a SWAT team, bungling terrorists, photo-snapping tourists, Gary the Gorilla, and a TV news reporter. After prehistoric-size mishaps and a talk with the President, Wally learns that maybe honesty really is the best policy.
(ISBN 0–8499–3537–7)

#6—My Life As a Torpedo Test Target

Wally uncovers the mysterious secrets of a sunken submarine. As dreams of fame and glory increase, so do the famous McDoogle mishaps. Besides hostile sea creatures, hostile pirates, and hostile Wally McDoogle clumsiness, there is the war against his own greed and selfishness. It isn't until Wally finds himself on a wild ride atop a misguided torpedo that he realizes the source of true greatness.
(ISBN 0–8499–3538–5)

Look for this humorous fiction series
at your local Christian bookstore.